MICHELLE VERNAL LOVES a happy ending. She lives with her husband and their two boys in the beautiful and resilient city of Christchurch, New Zealand. She's partial to a glass of wine, loves a cheese scone, and has recently taken up yoga—a sight to behold indeed. As well as The Guesthouse on the Green series Michelle's written six novels. They're all written with humour and warmth and she hopes you enjoy reading them. If you enjoy O'Mara's then taking the time to say so by leaving a review would be wonderful. A book review is the best present you can give an author. If you'd like to hear about new releases in this series, and Michelle's writing news you can sign up to receive her Newsletter at: www.michellevernal.books.com

To say thank you, you'll receive an exclusive character profile of the O'Mara women!

# The Guesthouse on the Green
# O'Mara's
# Michelle Vernal

THE RED FOX POKED HIS head through the hole he'd dug under the bricks. This was his secret point of entry. A closely guarded gap between the brick wall separating the gardens in which he had his den and his favourite dustbin.

The bin was located around the back of a handsome Georgian townhouse, one of a long row of identical buildings opposite St Stephen's Green. This particular bin with its scraps of bacon, black and white pudding, sausage, fried potato, toast crusts, and on occasion, soda bread had the best pickings in the area.

His ears were pricked for any sounds alerting him to danger and his black nose twitched as he sniffed the night air. It was crisp with a tang of chimney smoke and the remnants of late-night suppers. The only sound was the odd car winding its lonely way home. He waited a beat or two longer and only when he was certain it was safe did he squeeze his bristly body through the gap.

The one and only time he'd been bold enough to investigate the bin's contents in the early morning hours, he'd encountered a fierce round woman, wielding a rolling pin. She'd shouted at him and waved that wooden baton in a way which meant to do him harm. Thankfully her cumbersome size meant she wasn't quick enough to catch him, and he'd shot back through his hole into the sanctity of his gardens—safe. He'd heard her muttering about setting a trap, but none had ever been laid. His prowess when it came to keeping the mice at bay, had been his saving grace. It had been a lesson learned, though, and calling as those first shards of morning light broke was a mistake he'd not made twice—until now.

His yellow eyes darted about the courtyard inspecting the shadowed corners. A chink of light peeped through the curtains of the room closest to the back door despite the lateness of the hour. The temptation of what he might find in the bin however was too strong. He couldn't turn back now, and he crept stealthily over to it, nudging at the lid with his nose. As he felt it budge, he was grateful it never sat as firmly over the lip as it should and with one last good push it slid off, clattering to the ground.

He had to move fast now, and he dived in head first emerging victoriously having snared a piece of bacon rind and a sausage. They would make a tasty addition to the grasses, berries, and odd squirrel he dined on in the gardens. The curtains to the room were wrenched open flooding the courtyard with light. The fox snaffled his rind and scrambled from the bin, jubilantly dragging the sausage he'd found with him. It would make for a feast to be enjoyed back in his den.

He glanced back to see how the land lay. A woman of indeterminable years stood at the window, her tear-stained face peering out into the courtyard. They were a strange lot these humans he thought, squeezing back through the cavity and slipping away into the darkness.

# Chapter 1
# 1999 Dublin

Aisling O'Mara had a gift. It hadn't been bestowed on her by three meddlesome fairies like Princess Aurora's gifts of beauty, song, and being awakened by her true love's kiss. Oh, she was an attractive enough woman, or so she'd been told on occasion. Marcus, whom she'd thought was her true love, used to give her an admiring once-over from time to time and tell her she was a fine-looking woman. He'd never been the effusive sort, but then again, he did work in banking.

As for beauty, well now it had bypassed her and blessed the face of her younger sister, Moira. She'd been Maureen O'Mara's 'surprise' baby. The day she arrived, Maureen told her husband, Brian, he could forget about giving her the glad eye in the future. She'd be keeping her legs crossed until the end of her days ta very much.

Aisling had been nine when she and Roisin, to their disgust, had to push their beds closer together so as to make way for their baby sister. Whether her sister's beauty was a gift, Aisling was unsure, because things came easily to Moira, far too easily, and she was headed for a fall. Aisling could feel it in her bones. She'd had the same feeling in the weeks leading up to her wedding, only she'd ignored it, more fool her.

So, that left song. Celine Dion, she was not. Shortly after her tenth birthday she'd auditioned for the children's choir at

St Teresa's and been told in not so many words, *don't call us, we'll call you*. Suffice to say they'd never called. Not even when mammy had tried to bribe the choirmaster with one of her famous Porter Cakes.

No, Aisling's gift was a simple one. There was no magic involved. Hers was a practical gift. She'd been born with an innate ability to listen to and fix other people's problems. *Talk to Aisling, she'll know what to do.* How many times had she heard that sentence uttered over the years? It was to her that family and friends turned when they needed a shoulder and sometimes it could be a heavy burden. Aisling often thought instead of managing the family's guesthouse, O'Mara's Manor House, she should have had a newspaper column. It would be called Dear Aisling or Ask Aisling. Not original titles by any means, but effective and straight to the point. She would be the Irish version of the agony aunt over in the States, what was her name? Dear Abby—that was it.

Yes, she sighed sipping her coffee and looking at the letter lying open on the table, her talents were wasted.

'I'm off now.' Moira popped her head around the doorway. 'Don't wait up for me tonight, I'll be late.' She strode over to the table and snatched a piece of Aisling's toast, stuffing the triangle into her mouth before Aisling could shriek at her to give it back.

Moira was employed as a receptionist for one of Ireland's largest law firms, Mason Price. Seeing how Friday had rolled around, Aisling knew Moira would be staying behind for the customary end of week drinks.

'If you got up earlier, you'd have time to make your own toast.'

'Yours tastes better.'

'It's toast not cordon bleu cooking.' Aisling took stock of her younger sibling, her mouth curving as she spied the white runners peeking out from under the hem of her black trousers. They were very Minnie Mouse, but Aisling knew as soon as Moira got to work, they'd be swapped for a pair of heels. As long as they weren't *her* heels.

'You've not got my black Miu Miu's in your bag, have you?' She stared hard at Moira whose left eye twitched when she fibbed.

'No, and would you leave off about your stupid Miu Miu's. I borrowed them once.'

'And got a scratch on the heel.'

'It was microscopic.' Moira's hand snaked out for another piece of toast, but Aisling was quicker and held the plate up out of her reach. She hadn't detected a twitching eye; she'd let the Miu Miu's go for now. It made sense for Moira to walk the short distance to the multi-storey office building near the Grand Canal. The traffic was bumper to bumper of a morning and it was faster to get there on foot.

Moira looked particularly lovely today, footwear aside, with her dark hair scooped back into a low ponytail. The moss green coloured blouse she was wearing under her suit jacket brought out the flecks of gold in her hazel eyes. To be fair, the black Miu Miu's would have worked a treat with her sister's black trousers.

Moira and their older sister Roisin both took after their mammy. They'd inherited her olive skin which obligingly turned mahogany when they went on their holidays. Aisling had Nanna Dee on their dad's side, long gone now bless the old harridan, to thank for her strawberry blonde mop. The green eyes, a smattering of freckles, and skin that refused to tan no matter how long she sat out in the sun, meant she'd drawn the short straw in her opinion. Not that she got much opportunity for sunbathing these days anyway, and it wasn't just down to Dublin's inclement weather.

Aisling couldn't remember the last time she'd taken a holiday. There'd been no opportunity for time off since she'd taken over the running of the guesthouse nearly two years ago. It was a job that needed her at the helm seven days a week, three hundred and sixty-five days of the year. Of course, Moira, Mammy, and Roisin would argue this wasn't the case. They'd be quick to say Aisling *chose* to see herself as indispensable. Perhaps it was true. She needed to keep herself busy after everything that had happened. God, she'd had a hell of a twelve months.

# Chapter 2

'Ash, did you hear me?' Moira waved a hand in front of her sister's face.

'What? Oh yes, you said you'll be late. Well, have fun, but don't go getting hammered or anything.'

This received a frown. 'You're such a sourpuss these days and you're not my keeper, Aisling O'Mara. I'm twenty-five, not fifteen.'

Aisling sighed, she never used to be a sourpuss. 'Sorry. It's habit, but we've got lunch with Mammy tomorrow remember, and you don't want a sore head or you'll never hear the end of it from her.'

'Oh, feck it, I'd forgotten all about that,' said Moira. I've arranged to meet Andrea on Grafton Street for eleven o'clock tomorrow. I was really looking forward to it too. We're going shopping. I'm due some retail therapy.'

Money burned a hole in her sister's pocket. Aisling decided she was allowed to be self-righteous. She'd managed to kick her designer-shoe shopping habit when she'd arrived back in Dublin. Marcus and his thrifty ways had seen to that. Truth be told she hadn't had much choice in the matter, a disposable income was needed to maintain a designer-shoe habit. The wage she drew from O'Mara's, while a living one, was not a patch on her old salary. The old Aisling had packed up her frivolous side when she'd packed her bags and returned to O'Mara's after Dad got sick.

'Don't roll your eyes, Ash. I *need* a new dress because Posh Mairead from the Finance Department's gotten engaged to Niall. He's a senior partner, and how she snared him with those buck teeth of hers I don't know—there's hope for us all. Personally, I think he's only marrying her because of her family name. The Horan's are old money, and everybody knows Mairead only works because her daddy thought it would be good for her to see how the other half live. Anyway, the engagement party's only a couple of weeks away and I've got absolutely nothing to wear. I have to look my best because all the partners have been invited and I have it on good authority Liam Shaughnessy from Asset Management is going to be there.'

Aisling was exhausted by the time Moira finished her monologue but not so tired she hadn't seen the predatory gleam in her eyes as she mentioned Liam Shaughnessy. 'Be careful, Moira,' she warned for the second time that morning.

'What?'

'From what you've told me, yer man, Liam, sounds like a player.'

'Ash, just because you made a bad call doesn't mean all men are tarred with the same brush as Marcus fecking coward McDonagh. He was a selfish eejit.' She shuddered for effect. 'I didn't like the way he'd give you that look.'

'What look?'

'The look that said you were being loud. It made me want to kick him. It was the same look Mr Mathias used to give me in the juniors. He always described me as a disruptive member of the class. I wanted to kick him too remember?'

'Vaguely.' Alright, so Marcus didn't like her drawing attention to herself but that was because he was reserved. He liked to sit back and observe not be thrown in the mix.

'And the way that man used to hog the remote control for the tele spoke volumes, an only child, used to getting his own way.'

Aisling looked at her sister. She'd forgotten how he did that. The channel surfing had driven her mad. She'd be happily involved in Melrose Place and the next she'd be confronted by that mad Australian wrestling crocodiles. An annoying habit she'd add to her list of reasons as to why she should continue ignoring his letters. Maybe Moira was right when she said she was bitter from having been burned. She was bitter like an unripe lemon.

'Anyway,' Moira prattled on, 'Mairead's only gone and hired The Saddle Room at the Shelbourne for it.' She breathed, 'Shelbourne' with reverence before looking hopefully at Aisling. 'Maybe you could explain to Mammy for me? Sure look it, we could always make it for the following week.'

'I will not. You've got plenty of things you can wear. Your wardrobe's overflowing as it is. Mammy doesn't ask a lot from us, Moira, you know that.' Seeing Moira open her mouth she warded her off. 'Alright, I'll grant you she tells us what to do a lot, but she's had such a horrible time of it, the least you can do is front up for lunch. She looks forward to seeing us.'

'We've all had a horrible fecking time,' Moira huffed. 'And it's bloody inconvenient. She's a whirling social dervish that fits us in to suit *her* social calendar.' Moira's hazel eyes regarded her sister steadily. 'And don't start because it's true and you know it.'

She could be a selfish mare sometimes thought Aisling as she shut her mouth. They would go to lunch to keep the peace even if she did have a point.

'What's that you've got there?' Moira pointed to the letter lying next to Aisling's plate, her face lighting up as she asked, 'Is it from Pat?'

Moira adored Patrick, their handsome big brother. Aisling, however, had his number. Although, she was the only one in the family who did. He was a chancer. Mammy thought the sun shone out of her eldest child and only son's arse. She could make an excuse for his behaviour faster than a magician could pull a rabbit out of a hat. Roisin sat on the fence. She'd side with Mammy and Moira when it suited and agree with Aisling when she wanted to borrow a pair of her shoes.

Patrick O'Mara was a selfish so-and-so with notions about himself. Look at how he'd thrown his toys out of the cot after Dad died. He'd flown off to the States without a backward glance when he hadn't got his way over O'Mara's being sold, right when Mammy needed him most. Aisling frowned. As far as she was concerned, America wasn't far enough. Her brother always had his own best interests at heart. If he was chocolate, he'd eat himself.

'No, not Patrick, it's from the ESB that's all, gas is going up again.' The lie tripped smoothly from her tongue and she felt a flash of anger towards Patrick as she saw the look of disappointment on her sister's face. He hadn't been in touch since Christmas, and then he'd only sent a card and a photograph of himself and his new girlfriend, Cindy. She was the perfect appendage. Arm candy with big blonde hair and a perfectly aligned, white, toothy smile. Moira, upon seeing the photograph fall from his

Christmas card, had announced, *her boobs weren't gifted to her by God that's for sure.*

'That reminds me I forgot to tell you, Roisin rang yesterday,' Aisling said. 'Noah's getting a certificate for 'good work' at his school assembly this morning.'

Their nephew had only started at his primary school in the affluent London suburb of Highgate a month ago and was already getting a pat on the back. Aisling felt a surge of pride as though she personally had something to do with him being awarded an accolade. There'd be no hope for her in years to come if he went on to graduate from university.

Moira's smile was wistful. 'Ah, I wish we could be there cheering him on. His little face will be a picture. Mind you Colin the Arse will be puffed up like a peacock saying it's down to the Quealey genes, eejit that he is. Do yer know the last time I spoke to Roisin, she told me he'd got it in his head that Noah's the next Beckham, because he scored a goal at toddler footie. I'll bet you anything, he's one of those awful parents who stands on the side-lines shouting and bawling.' Her mouth formed a startled 'O' as the old grandfather clock in the corner chimed the half hour. 'Feck is that the time? I've got to run or I'll be late.'

A twinkling later their front door banged as Moira left and no doubt hurtled down the stairs two at a time. Hurricane Moira. If Mammy had been here, Aisling knew she'd have called after her, *Slow and steady wins the race, Moira!* She was full of pertinent idioms. Aisling wondered at times whether she kept a book hidden about her person so as to always have the right saying on hand at the right moment!

Alone once more Aisling turned her attention back to the letter she'd been reading before her sister appeared. She kept returning to it. It was rather like picking at a scab for want of a nicer turn of phrase. The plain white envelope it had arrived in a few days earlier had been addressed in the handwriting that always sent a piercing stab straight through her heart. She picked it up from where she'd leaned it against the salt shaker and eyed the carefully written address for a few moments.

How much easier things would have been if she could have packed her bags and run far away when it happened. Preferably somewhere warm with balmy breezes and coconut palms, lots of coconut palms. She shivered it was nothing a hot shower wouldn't fix.

Aisling folded the letter, placing it back inside the envelope, before pushing her chair back and getting up from the table. She tucked it away in the hidden drawer at the back of the bureau where Mammy used to stuff the letters that came from the hospital. It was as if she'd believed by ignoring the information they contained she could make what was happening to her husband go away. These days there was a new pile of letters there which Aisling wished she could make go away. She locked the drawer, returning the key to its hook on the inside of the desk. Her talents were wasted she thought, for the second time that morning mentally composing a Dear Aisling letter.

*Dear Aisling,*

*I was due to get married this time last year only my fiancé disappeared a week before our wedding. He left me with no explanation as to why he'd left other than a brief note saying he was sorry, but he couldn't go through with the wedding. Three months ago, he began writing to me from Cork, his bolthole asking me to for-*

*give him. He says it was all a huge mistake, he got cold feet, and*
*he wants a second chance. Blah, blah, blah. What should I do?*
  *Yours faithfully,*
  *Me*

The problem was, while she was a wonder at sorting out the lives of those around her, Aisling didn't have the foggiest how to fix what was wrong in hers.

Aisling shook her head in an effort to clear it. Marcus fecking coward McDonagh, as Moira so charmingly referred to him, didn't deserve to occupy any more of her thoughts today. With that, she banished him and moved over to the windows. The sky, she saw, drawing the curtains and hooking them back, was pale blue with fat scudding clouds. A cool wind had been blowing most of the week. Still, it wasn't raining; that was something.

She stared through the panes of glass. There were six of them in total. She could recall their mammy effing and blinding when it was time to give them a good polish. Now the job fell to her she knew how Mammy had felt, they were a sod to clean. Across the road, the leafy tops of the trees in St Stephen's Green danced as they tried to cling valiantly to the boughs.

Autumn had always been Aisling's favourite time of the year. She loved to watch the greenery give way to the fiery oranges, reds, and yellows of autumn. Since Marcus had left, the season had lost its allure. Now it was a reminder that a year ago she'd been jilted. Her gaze dropped to the traffic on the road below.

It was heavy with the early morning rush, people hurrying here, there, and everywhere. The streets were so congested these days. She was glad she didn't have to travel far to work—three flights of stairs down to reception and she was there. And on that note, she thought, moving away from the window, it was time she got her a into g. O'Mara's was mad busy of a Friday with the influx of travellers arriving for the weekend. Aisling liked to keep on the go; being busy was an all too welcome distraction from Marcus.

# Chapter 3

'Morning, Aisling,' Bronagh Hanrahan mumbled. 'Love the suit, very you.' Her mouth was full as she looked up from the computer where she was processing a reservation with one hand and holding a spoon in the other. It was something she could do with her eyes closed given how long she'd worked for the O'Mara's—nearly thirty years! Mind you, when Maureen O'Mara had first gotten the Macintosh, Bronagh had been dragged kicking and screaming into the computer age. A mug of tea was next to the keyboard along with a bowl of cereal, Bronagh's requisite box of Special K next to her in tray.

Bronagh was a serial dieter and could often be heard lamenting no matter how hard she tried, she couldn't seem to lose any weight. 'It's the menopause, so it is. It gets us all in the end,' she'd state before pointing a finger. 'Just you wait, Aisling. You'll hit your forties and that lovely slim waist of yours will vanish and you'll be left with a roll around your middle like that short bald fella's.'

'What short bald fella?'

'Ah, you know, yer man, the Buddha chap.'

This amused Aisling because she knew, were she to open the drawer in the desk at which Bronagh sat, she'd find a half-eaten packet of custard cream's in there. It also surprised her to hear her waist being referred to as slim. She'd always been the well-padded one in the family. There was nothing like a broken heart to curb one's appetite though, and the pounds had fallen off her in the weeks after the wedding was cancelled.

Aisling greeted Bronagh, confiding in her that while her shoes had cost the earth, the suit had been a steal at Penneys. She was a firm believer in anything looking a million dollars so long as it was paired with the right shoes. It was how she justified the ludicrous sums she'd splurged on them over the years.

She peered over Bronagh's shoulder and ran a finger down the diary's open page to see who was checking out that morning. Their receptionist might be au fait with the Mac, but she still didn't trust it and insisted on keeping all their guests logged in her diary as well. Behind them the fax whirred into life and began churning its message out as the phone simultaneously began to ring. Aisling grinned as Bronagh's jaw went into overdrive before she swallowed and composed herself.

'Good morning, O'Mara's Manor House, you're speaking with Bronagh. How can I help?'

Ever the professional. Aisling was still smiling as a commotion sounded on the stairs a second later. Her head swivelled in that direction. Mr Miller, larger-than-life, was standing on the landing. His suitcase was beside him, as was a large holdall. He had a baseball style cap pulled down on his head, his t-shirt bore the slogan "Kansas: *Not Everything is Flat*", and a camera was slung around his neck. He was urging his wife to get a move on, in his booming Midwestern American accent.

'June-bug, for the love of God, woman, get down here! I can't carry all of this on my own.'

'I'm coming, Jacob, don't rush me. You know I hate being rushed.'

'Can I help with anything, Mr Miller?' Aisling moved over to the base of the stairs looking up at him as she rested a hand on the rail, ready to go to his aid.

'You could put a rocket up my wife, Aisling, that would help. The tour bus will be stopping by to pick us up any minute.' He gestured to the holdall. 'Do you think you could manage that? This case weighs a ton. June's been shopping for the kids and the grandkids, as well as half of Kansas City, and we're only three days into our tour.'

Aisling made her way up to the first-floor landing, taking the bag and hefting it up over her shoulder. Mrs Miller had proudly displayed all her treasures in the guest lounge for her to admire last night. She'd made the appropriate enthusiastic noises as the American woman had shaken a glass dome demonstrating how snow fell on the little leprechaun trapped inside. She'd bought tea towels with four-leaf clovers and Irish blessings printed on them, along with a Foster and Allen CD. She had a selection of thimbles, wishing jars, and luck stones. Her precious Belleek pottery was bubble-wrapped but Aisling hoped the delicate china didn't break between now and when she arrived home.

Mrs Miller's pride and joy though, she declared, was a traditional Irish dancing costume. It had come complete with a red ringlet wig. 'I did Irish dancing as a girl, Aisling, and I always wanted the proper dress and shoes to wear. There was no money for frivolities when I was a young'un though—not with eight mouths to feed in the family.'

Aisling had bitten her bottom lip to stop herself envisaging the well-endowed Mrs Miller jigging about in her short green dress, white tights, and black shoes to her Foster and Allen CD, reliving her childhood dream. Each to their own!

'I checked out already, so once my wife decides to grace us with her presence, we're good to go. Ah, speak of the devil. Here she comes.'

June Miller's tread sounded lightly on the stairs and she appeared behind her husband. 'It was my hair, Aisling,' she said spotting her. 'Flat as a pancake after I blow-dried it this morning. The water's so soft here. I looked like I had a helmet on and I've been trying to zhoosh it up a bit.'

'Well, you succeeded. You look like you stuck your finger in an electric socket, woman. You should have left it alone.'

He wasn't wrong, but Aisling gave her a reassuring smile. 'It looks lovely, Mrs Miller. There's loads of body in it. Now then, I hear you've got a bus to be catching. So we'd best get down these stairs.'

The couple, cases thudding behind them, followed her down to the foyer where a tall, thin man in a tweed cap and clobber that would look right at home on a farm in County Middle-of-Nowhere, had appeared.

'Ah, here they are now,' said Bronagh.

'Mr and Mrs Miller?' the man said, stepping forward.

Mr Miller took his outstretched hand and shook it. 'Please call me Jacob and this is my wife June.'

The man nodded and smiled at June, revealing a missing front tooth before taking her suitcase from her.

Jaysus! Aisling wondered what the tour company was called, Boondocks Bus Breaks, perhaps?

'I'm your tour guide, Ruaraidh. The bus is outside.'

'Say your name again, son?'

'Ruaraidh.'

'I think I'll just call you Roy, if that's okay.'

Jacob Miller didn't wait for a reply, turning his attention to Aisling and Bronagh. 'Thank you, ladies, for your wonderful hospitality. We've enjoyed every minute of our time here in your capital city haven't we, June? It's a fine establishment you run, Aisling.'

'We sure have. You made us so welcome. We appreciate it, and we'll spread the word about your beautiful manor house won't we, Jacob?'

'We will indeedy.'

This was what it was all about, giving their guests happy memories of their time here in Dublin. Aisling thanked them both for their kind words and for staying with them, before wishing them a fabulous time tripping around Ireland.

Ruaraidh moved toward the door eager to get his two charges on board the bus. Aisling tried not to laugh at the look on his face as Mr Miller boomed, 'Lead the way, Roy, my boy.'

'Enjoy the craic!' Bronagh called after them.

There was a whoosh of cool air as Ruaraidh opened the door and they heard Mrs Miller lament as she stepped outside. 'Darn it, Jacob, if you hadn't been rushing me, I would have put a scarf over my hair. That wind will flatten it faster—'

'Oh, put a sock in it, woman.'

Any further exchange was lost as the door shut behind them. Bronagh and Aisling grinned at each other. There were some guests who made you laugh, the Millers a case in point, and some that made you pull your hair out. Aisling threw a glance over her shoulder to Room 1. It was the only room on the ground floor, a single, and given the courtyard outlook, its nightly rate was cheaper than their other nine rooms. The door was firmly shut.

Miss Brennan had complained about other guests keeping her awake with their chatter in the lounge. The guest lounge was behind reception to the left and the stairs were all that separated Room 1 from it, but no one had complained about the noise being a problem before. She'd also complained about the foot traffic up and down the stairs of a morning as other guests made their way down to the dining room below for breakfast.

She'd only been here for two nights and had found something to moan about each morning. Aisling wondered what today's problem would be. Then she frowned, remembering what Moira had called her this morning, a sourpuss. She didn't want to be like Miss Brennan. She'd always had a positive outlook on life and had been rewarded for this with a good life. It had been marching along in the direction she'd thought it would—the altar. Marcus had snatched her happy-go-lucky attitude away though. He'd shattered not only her trust but her heart too. *Stop it Aisling, don't go there.*

She focussed on the diary instead and flicked a couple of pages until she found what she was looking for. Their problematic guest wasn't checking out until Monday, three more days! Her mother's old mantra ran through her head, *Just like the customer's always right, Aisling, our guests are always right. Even when they're not!*

It was this attitude toward the people that chose to stay at O'Mara's that had turned it around from a tired old manor house and establishment that had seen better days to the quaint but plush accommodation offered today. So Aisling resolved no matter what Miss Una Brennan from County Waterford pulled out of her hat this morning, she would smile sweetly and promise to sort the problem for her. Just as well it was she and not Moira who'd stepped up and taken over running the guest house. Her sister had never mastered the art of smiling sweetly. She'd be likely to tell the old wagon—the particularly Irish epithet reserved for the most awkward of their female guests was a favourite of her sister's—that the tide wouldn't take her out, or that the sea wouldn't give her a wave or some such insult.

Smiling at the thought of what Moira with her repertoire of sharp retorts would say she set about her morning routine. It began with a customary sweep of reception to take note of what needed a tidy up. The phone was ringing once more, and Aisling left Bronagh to answer it. The cushions on the elegant rolled arm sofa with its cream and green stripes could do with a plump. She saw to those first before straightening the magazines on the antique mahogany coffee table. A few of the brochures were out, and she refilled the Wicklow Tours slot with the glossy Slane Castle pamphlets ensuring there were no empty spaces.

There were only two of Quinn's flyers advertising his restaurant of the same name left. It was as good an excuse as any to call on him. Not that she needed an excuse! She'd known Quinn and had been firm friends with him since their wayward student days.

Maybe, she'd even take him up on his offer of dinner on the house. His way of saying thank you for recommending his traditional Irish fare to their guests. It would be nice not to cook for a change. Moira's culinary skills were limited so unless Aisling wanted to dine on beans on toast each night, preparing the evening meal fell to her.

Yes, she decided, once breakfast was finished, she'd stroll over to Quinn's. Her eyes roved over the stand one last time and when she was satisfied all was shipshape, she turned her attention to the blooms on top of the front desk. Bronagh, she saw was off the phone and scraping out the remnants from her breakfast bowl.

The bouquet arrived fresh from Fi's Florists once a fortnight on a Monday morning. They'd need a freshen up if they were to continue looking their best between now and then. Aisling knew the tricks of the trade, trim the stems and add a little sugar to the water. She picked up the vase and carried it out to the poky but 'sufficient for their needs' kitchenette at the very back on the ground floor. The door beside it held a chunky old-fashioned brass key which when turned allowed the door to open up onto the steps outside. They led down to the concreted courtyard. Nobody used it, nobody except Mr Fox and Mrs Flaherty when she took out the rubbish.

The little red fox was rarely seen but often heard as he checked out what had gone into the bin that day. His calling card was the rubbish he'd leave strewn about the courtyard. Their breakfast cook, Mrs Flaherty, who despite her rosy apple cheeks, and pensionable age could drop the 'f' bomb with the best of them was often heard shrieking, *That fecking fox!* Ita in charge of housekeeping was terrified of her and Aisling wished she had the same effect on the young woman because she might actually do some work then.

There was no need for a garden at the rear of the house for two reasons. Firstly, St Stephen's Green was their front garden. Sure there was a busy road separating them from the Green, but it was only a hop, skip, and a jump away. Secondly, the back wall of O'Mara's housed a secret. A gate which, if ventured through, welcomed you into the Iveagh Gardens, Mr Fox's home.

Aisling took the flowers, their scent still heady, from the vase and set about her task. It was in this little kitchenette that Bronagh would heat up her leftover dinner for lunch or make herself a cup of tea. She was on the front desk from eight am until four pm Monday to Friday and then Nina the young Spanish girl who'd started a year ago would arrive to do the evening shift. Of a weekend, James and Evie, two students, split the front desk shifts. Aisling spent her days overseeing them all.

Satisfied the arrangement would continue to brighten reception until Fi's next delivery, she carried the vase back to the front desk. The guest lounge was next on her agenda. It was her favourite room in the whole house. Aisling loved the cosy, yet elegant sunny space. She'd conjure up images of the well-heeled people who'd have been received there when it had served as a drawing room. The ladies she pictured all looked suspiciously like they'd stepped from the pages of a Jane Austen novel and the men bore an uncanny resemblance to Colin Firth as Mr Darcy.

She stood in the doorway of the lounge for a moment. Her mammy had combed the antique markets for the furnishings in here including the gilt framed artworks that lined the walls. The light flooded in through twin floor-to-ceiling windows in keeping with the era of the house. The original fireplace was nestled between the windows. It was laid, but never used these days thanks to the wonders of central heating. She liked to envisage the visitors of old gathering around that fire in the wintertime as it roared and spat, with a glass of something warming and welcoming in their hand.

Aisling fluffed the cushions on the three-seater sofa identical to the lounger in reception. She straightened the magazines on the coffee table before checking the milk pottles and tea and coffee sachets in the tray on top of the buffet opposite.

The Earl Grey teabags needed replenishing; they were always popular and, opening the cupboard, she took out the box and refilled them. Next in her morning routine was the room freshener. She spritzed each morning walking around the expansive room giving it a couple of bursts. If she closed her eyes, she could imagine she was in a grassy meadow, but without being afflicted by hay fever!

A teacup sat on the coffee table with a ring of red lipstick around the rim and picking it up she took it out to the kitchenette to wash. She'd draped the tea towel over the rail and had decided to pop downstairs to see how the land lay with Mrs Flaherty this morning when the door to Room 1 opened.

# Chapter 4

'Oh, good morning, Miss Brennan. I trust you slept well.' Aisling tried to keep the note of hope from her voice. She could hear Mammy's voice in her ear, *She's the sort if you give her an inch, she'll take a mile.* Mammy might not be here, but she was right. Miss Brennan was a woman who'd sense weakness and exploit it and from the tight-lipped look Aisling was receiving now, it seemed she already had.

'I didn't as it happens. There was a dreadful carry-on outside my window in the small hours.'

Aisling silently cursed Mr Fox wishing he could have chosen to raid someone else's bin last night. 'I'm so sorry Miss Brennan. That would be our resident fox. He comes a calling from the Iveagh Gardens, they're behind the wall to the rear of the house. She donned her brightest smile and told herself to rise above Miss Brennan's pettiness and find something nice to say. She was going to have to dig deep.

'That blue's such a lovely colour on you.' It was true actually. The pale blue blouse Una Brennan wore under her cardigan was the same shade as her eyes. She'd have been pretty once, but now her features were pinched. Her face spoke of an internal unhappiness, and the harsh line of her tight bun from which a few silver curls escaped did nothing to soften her appearance. 'Are you on your way to breakfast?' Aisling didn't expect an acknowledgement of her compliment.

'I am. I hope it doesn't take as long as it did yesterday. I think the cook was waiting for the hen to lay the egg. I've an appointment at ten o'clock this morning.'

'We do have the continental option available if you're in a hurry, Miss Brennan.'

'I prefer a cooked breakfast.' And with that, the older woman marched off down the stairs.

*Awkward so-and-so.* Aisling would put money on her having been a headmistress or something of the like in her younger days. Her cardigan and skirt ensemble teamed with sensible shoes reminded her of the bad-tempered English teacher she'd had in secondary school. She stole a glance at her own impractical but oh so pretty Walter Steiger shoes as she recalled the awful woman. She used to frisbee the school books across the room to her students. She'd also had a habit of slamming her ruler down on the desk of any pupil who looked like they might be daydreaming about their latest favourite pop star rather than conjugating their verbs. Given Aisling had been smitten with Jon Bon Jovi that year, her desk had gotten a hammering! Now she poked her tongue out at Miss Brennan's retreating back. Mammy wouldn't approve but Mammy wasn't here.

~

There were a handful of people seated at the tables Aisling saw as she descended the stairs to the basement dining room. They were laid with white cloths and silver cutlery. Mr and Mrs Freeman from Australia with their teenage sons were tucking in to their breakfast. They'd obviously risen bright and early. The family had toured Britain and had tagged on Ireland for the last two weeks of their holiday. The younger of the two brothers had finished high school and this was a last hurrah before he too flew the nest and went off to university, Mrs Freeman had confided in Aisling.

The boys, who looked alike apart from their haircuts were seated at a separate table to their parents. Aisling watched for a second as they shovelled down their bacon and eggs like they hadn't seen food since leaving Australia. It made her smile as she remembered Mammy going on about Patrick having hollow legs when he was a teen.

Her gaze flicked over to the young couple from Cork, the Prestons. They were seated in the far corner of the room beneath a large black and white print of Grafton Street in the twenties. Upon hearing they were from Cork, Aisling had been tempted to flash them a photo of Marcus. She wanted to ask if they'd seen him, and if so, how did he look? It was a crazy thought, but then sometimes where he was concerned, she felt as though she had indeed gone crazy.

She'd managed to reign herself in and had learned that the reason behind the Prestons' visit was down to his being courted by the Dublin branch of the firm he worked at. The company had high hopes of tempting him and his wife to relocate to the Fair City. By the looks of their clean plates they'd enjoyed their breakfast and were savouring a cup of tea before getting on with whatever the day had in store for them.

The retired and portly Mr Walsh, who'd left Dublin for Liverpool many moons ago was seated at a table near the door to the kitchen. He was buttering his toast and casting about the table. He was missing Mrs Flaherty's homemade marmalade Aisling guessed, and she ducked on through to the kitchen to spoon some into a dish for him.

'Good morning,' she greeted Mrs Flaherty, whose cheeks were even pinker than usual thanks to the heat from the frying pan, and received a nod in return. Aisling wasn't offended, one didn't disturb Mrs Flaherty when she was near a hot stove. She set about scraping the chunky orange marmalade from the jar into a dish and, leaving the cook to her bacon and black pudding, she carried it through.

'Here we go, Mr Walsh. I think this is what you were missing.' She set the dish down.

'Aisling, pet, you're a wonder.'

'Well now if I didn't know how partial you were to Mrs Flaherty's marmalade after all the years you've been coming to stay, I'd be a poor hostess indeed.' Mr Walsh had been booking in to his favourite room on the third floor of O'Mara's for five nights in the first week of September for as long as Aisling could remember. He had a standing order to come back each year to visit his older sister who lived in Rathmines. She'd never married he'd told Aisling once and had never moved from what had been their family home. He refused to stay with her despite her living in the house he'd grown up in because he said she drove him batty!

'Will you join me?' He gestured to his teapot. Mr Walsh liked her to sit down and share a cuppa with him of a morning. He reckoned her and Bronagh were the only sane people he spoke to once he left O'Mara's for the day.

'Give me two ticks,' she smiled. It faltered as she spied Miss Brennan. She'd settled herself as far away from the other guests as she could manage. Aisling wondered what her problem was. What made a person so cantankerous? She was spared from pondering her question by Mr Freeman waving her over.

'Good morning, Mr Freeman, what can I do for you?'

'So you really don't say 'Top of the morning to ye' then?'

'Only in the films, Mr Freeman. Do you say, hmm let me see—strewth?'

He winked. 'Fair dinkum, I do.'

Aisling laughed, 'Your gas.'

'Gas! I shall add that to my repertoire of Irish sayings.' His eyes twinkled as he went back to dipping his toast in his egg.

'Aisling,' Mrs Freeman said. 'We're going to see Riverdance tonight.'

It amused Aisling hearing one of her sons groan at the thought of an evening watching Irish dancing. His mother ignored him. 'We thought we'd have an early dinner before the show. Is there anywhere you recommend?'

'There is actually. I know of a lovely place just around the corner from here where the craic is great.' She grinned, seeing Mr Freeman sound out the word. 'It's called Quinn's and they serve traditional Irish fare in a cosy setting. The food's delicious. Would you like me to make a reservation for you?'

'That would be wonderful, thank you.'

'Say five-thirty? Would that give you enough time before the show?'

'What do you think, honey?'

Mr Freeman nodded. 'Bang on.'

It was funny hearing Irishisms in such a broad Australian accent Aisling thought giving him a thumbs up.

'Five-thirty would be perfect.'

'Five-thirty it is, Mrs Freeman. Mr Freeman, hoo-roo.' He roared with laughter. 'You got me with that one.'

She left them to get back to their breakfast, heading over to clear the Cork couple's plates. 'How was everything?' she asked stacking the two plates.

'Lovely, thank you. Mrs Flaherty's soda bread is better than my nana's but don't tell her I said that,' Mr Preston chuckled.

As she carried the dishes out to the kitchen, Aisling hoped Miss Brennan had overheard his high praise. She stacked the dirty dishes in the dishwasher and then retrieving an extra cup and saucer, went to join Mr Walsh, hearing Mrs Flaherty muttering behind her as she did so.

As she sat down opposite him, the cook pushed through the swinging door. She wiped her hands on her apron, her buttonlike blue eyes narrowed and her ample bosom heaving as she drew breath. She looked as though she were going into battle, a plump Boudica as she strode fearlessly across the dining room. Her voice rang out loudly as she asked Miss Brennan what she would like this morning.

Aisling turned her attention to Mr Walsh who set about pouring the tea as he told her all about his mad sister's refusal to throw anything out. 'She's got that much gear piled up in there she could open a junk shop because most of it is rubbish.'

Aisling relaxed listening to his banter, she liked his Liverpudlian accent. Mrs Flaherty was more than capable of handling the likes of Una Brennan.

# Chapter 5

U na eyed Aisling for a moment. Why she felt the need to totter about the place as though she were about to hit the runways of Paris was beyond her. They were in a Dublin guesthouse for goodness sake. An upmarket one, but a guesthouse, nevertheless. She turned away and cut a sliver of her white pudding, spearing it with her fork. She could sense that formidable cook hovering and she knew Aisling was wary of her. She'd been a short-tempered old bite but she couldn't help herself. She put her fork down.

The pudding was golden and looked crisp to the bite. It was cooked just the way she liked it and the only reason she wasn't relishing the full Irish breakfast on the plate in front of her was because her stomach was in knots. It had been from the moment she'd packed her bags and left her little terraced house in Ferrybank to board the Waterford to Dublin train. It had only worsened as the train chugged closer to the city and it was this that was making her ill-tempered.

She'd caught the bus from Heuston Station to St Stephen's Green and had peered out the window unsure of what to expect. Dublin was the city of her birth. She was born in 1932 the year of the world's largest Eucharistic Congress. Una's mam had talked of a live broadcast from Pope Pius XI all the way from Vatican City to Phoenix Park at the Sunday mass. Imagine that, she used to say, his voice travelling all the way from

Vatican City! She wondered what her mam would have made of the internet had she lived long enough for its invention.

It had been fifty years since Una had last walked the streets of this city. Back then she'd known them like the back of her hand. From what she could see not much had changed. The layout was still the same; she'd be able to find her way around despite the addition of the big, shiny glass monstrosities, so-called progress. What had changed, she'd sensed from the moment she stepped off the train, was the atmosphere. There was a buoyancy in people's steps that hadn't been here when she was a girl. The faces she passed as her case bumped along behind her weren't set in a hard, grim line of scraping by. There was a buzz in the air, lots of foreign accents, and the foot traffic! Well, it had to be seen to be believed. The streets were alive with activity.

She watched a double-decker bus pass by. The moss green buses of her youth that had belched their way around the streets with their open platform at the back were long gone. She recalled Leo leaping from that platform as the bus slowed despite the conductor's warning and he'd held his hand out to her daring her to do the same. She'd put her trust in him and taken a leap of faith.

Her decision to book into O'Mara's had been deliberate. She remembered the old guest house from her younger days. She'd walk past it each morning on her way to where she was employed as a secretary for an accountant. What a funny little man Mr Hart had been with his round glasses and habit of reciting passages from James Joyce's works at random. The work had been straightforward, and it had also afforded her enough money to pay her board to her mother. The small amount left aside went towards her and Leo's wedding fund.

The job was dull though, certainly not what she'd imagined herself doing when she was a little girl full of big dreams. This was why as she passed by O'Mara's with its pretty window baskets and shiny nameplate, she liked to imagine all the glamorous lives led inside the grand old townhouse. The la-di-da ladies who'd graced the rooms inside the Georgian manor house wouldn't have had to scrimp and save for their weddings—the weekly treat, a fish and chip supper at Beshoff's.

Oh the stories those brick walls could tell! Now of a pensionable age, while not wealthy by any means, she was comfortable. She only had herself to look after, and that had meant she'd been able to put aside a tidy amount to ensure she didn't have to go without in her retirement. It was time she saw the inside O'Mara's for herself, there was nowhere else she wished to stay in Dublin—certainly not with her sister, Aideen. At the thought of Aideen, her stomach knotted further, and she put her fork down.

'Is everything alright, Miss Brennan?'

Una was startled. She hadn't seen Mrs Flaherty approach her table once more, she'd been too lost in the past.

'I hope you're enjoying your white pudding. I buy in only the best from Brady's. They're craftsmen when it comes to stuffing their sausage casing.' The overbearing woman in her silly, frilly white apron challenged Una to disagree with her, her pudgy arms crossed over a ridiculously oversized bosom.

She didn't have the energy to be argumentative, not today. 'It's perfectly fine, thank you.' To prove her point, she picked up her fork and popped the pudding in her mouth. She was sure it was more than perfectly fine. She was sure it was sweet and creamy and delicious, but to her it tasted like sawdust. Nevertheless, she chewed resolutely willing Mrs Flaherty to bustle off back to where she'd come from.

The pantomime obviously satisfied the cook because with a curt, 'I'm glad you're enjoying it,' she waddled off back to the kitchen leaving her to dwell once more on what lay ahead today. There was no window to gaze out of here in the dining room. She supposed it would have once been used not just as the kitchen area, but for service and laundry too. Either way, the black and white photographs of bygone days in Dublin lining the walls weren't proving enough of a distraction.

Her mind wouldn't stop pondering how fifty years had passed so quickly. They had though, and Christmas after Christmas had rolled by without her spending it with her family. She'd always assumed she'd patch things up at some point but there had never been a right time. Sometimes it felt like she'd simply closed her eyes for a moment and when she'd opened them found herself transformed into the woman, she was now. Where had that girl whose future was mapped out as bright and shiny as a new penny vanished to? That girl had taken what she thought lay ahead for granted, hers for the taking. There'd be a handsome husband, children clinging to her skirts, and a house with an electric cooker and no outdoor privy! Instead, she was a woman with aches and pains, pushing seventy, who, if she were to be honest with herself, was lonely.

She'd vowed fifty years ago to never set foot in Dublin again. A promise she'd made in anger and one she hadn't felt able to shy away from until now.

# Chapter 6

The dining room began to empty, and Mr Walsh announced to Aisling he needed to get a move on too. Although, he confided, he'd much prefer to while away his day relaxing in O'Mara's with herself or the bonny Bronagh to keep him company. Oh yes, he lamented theatrically, if his time was his own, he'd happily whisk his favourite ladies across to the Green for a quiet meander around the gardens.

Aisling told him good-naturedly to get on his way and to be sure to pick up some cakes from the not long opened Queen of Tarts on Dame Street. 'It's out of your way but it's a lovely day for a walk, and if their chocolate fudge cake doesn't sweeten your sister, nothing will!' She sensed beneath all his bluster where his sister was concerned, there was an abiding affection. Why else would he come so religiously each year?

'Chocolate fudge cake you say?'

'The best chocolate fudge cake.'

He tapped the side of his nose before doffing his hat. 'Thanks for the tip, pet. I'll bring you a slice back.'

Aisling set about helping Mrs Flaherty clear the remaining tables—all the while listening to her mumblings about *that wagon of a woman*. Aisling assumed she was referring to Miss Brennan who'd barely touched her breakfast. She knew Mrs Flaherty always took it personally if food was left on a plate. By the time she'd moved on to her familiar monologue on *that fecking fox*, Aisling had begun to wipe the tables down. She glanced at the time, the breakfast service had another hour to run. By her count, there was only the businessman, in Room 7, and the Petersons in Room 3, who were yet to make an appearance. She promised Mrs Flaherty, as she always did, to do something about the fox while fully intending to do nothing. Their bin had been visited regularly of a night time for as long as Aisling could recall. If not by Mr Fox exactly then by his predecessors.

She'd seen him a handful of times, furtively edging his way across the courtyard before industriously nudging the bin lid off and helping himself to the day's leftovers. Sure, his untidy habits left a lot to be desired, but he did keep the mouse population down and she'd loved Roald Dahl's *Fantastic Mr Fox* as a child. The fox was staying.

'Aisling, go and check on that lazy lump, Ita. I can manage here now, I need to write my shopping list.'

Aisling knew when she was being dismissed and she knew better than to protest. Ita was supposed to be making up Room 9, the double Mr and Mrs Miller had vacated. The thought of geeing her up did not put a spring in her step as she climbed the stairs to the third floor. There was no lift in O'Mara's and for those that couldn't manage the stairs, Room 1 was the best option. Aisling reckoned running up and down between floors all day was more effective and economical than any gym. Her heels had the bonus of not just giving her several inches in height but giving her calves a jolly good workout too. If Mr Walsh kept his word and brought her back a slice of cake, she'd best pick up her pace.

The thought of gooey chocolate fudge cake revved her up and she wished, not for the first time, Ita would move at a quicker pace. Moira called her Idle Ita and it was fitting because, like Mrs Flaherty had just said, she did err on the side of laziness. Aisling strode down the corridor. A close eye had to be kept on her if the rooms were to be made up to O'Mara's high standard.

Ita Finnegan had worked at the guesthouse for just over two years. It had been her mammy who'd taken her on shortly before retiring from the business. Aisling would argue, given how sick their dad had been at the time, Mammy hadn't been in her right mind when Ita's mam, Kate, approached her. She and Maureen O'Mara were friends of old so when Kate asked Maureen if she could see her way to find something for Ita to do about the place, she'd felt obliged.

Aisling always got the impression from the younger girl she felt cleaning was beneath her. This was probably due to her insistence on not being referred to as the guesthouse's housekeeper. As it stood it was a job description Aisling thought undeserving, but Ita was adamant she be called by the more grandiose, *Director* of Housekeeping.

To be fair, she only kept her on because she hadn't done anything wrong per se and she hated the thought of having to give anyone their marching orders—especially not someone whose mam was friends with her mammy.

She wasn't good at confrontation. It came she reckoned from her position in the family. Patrick and Roisin had been the rabble rousers in their younger years, Moira the baby, and so it had fallen to her to be the peacemaker. Mind you, Ita sailed close to the wind at times, but Aisling knew too, given the current climate in the city, a replacement would not be easy to find. Jobs were plentiful, and beggars couldn't be choosers.

So, unless she wanted to take on the housekeeping role *and* explain herself to Mammy and Kate Finnegan, Ita, for the foreseeable future, was here to stay.

She found her sitting on the wingback chair by the window ignoring the gorgeous view of the Green as she leafed through a magazine. Mrs Miller must have left it behind. She jumped up from the chair when Aisling appeared in the doorway.

'Morning, Ita.' Aisling managed to bite back the snarky, 'hard at it, as usual, I see,' on the tip of her tongue.

'How're you, Aisling? I've done the bathroom and I was just about to sort the bed.' At least she had the grace to look sheepish as Aisling began pulling the sheets off it in an effort to galvanise her. It had the desired effect.

'Once you've finished in here, Ita, could you check on Rooms eight, six, four, and two, make sure they're all restocked, please? We're full occupancy tonight.' She shouldn't have to spell it out after all this time, but if she didn't their guests were likely to find themselves indisposed with no toilet paper!

Ita made a huffing noise as she balled the sheets and dumped them on the floor.

*Give me strength!* Aisling rolled her eyes and left her to it. Mammy had made a serious error in judgment when she took that one on. Friendship or no friendship.

~

'Bronagh, I'm going to call around to Quinn's. I promised the Freemans I'd make a reservation there for dinner this evening for them, and we're nearly out of his brochures.' She could have just telephoned and made the booking, but truth be told, she needed some fresh air. She was feeling irritated—Ita's snail-like pace always had that effect on her. Bronagh brushed the biscuit crumbs off her sweater and waved Aisling off.

'Be sure and tell Quinn I said hello.'

Bronagh had a soft spot for Quinn Moran, she got giggly and played with her hair a lot whenever he called. He was oblivious to her flirting, which only served to make her even more giggly. Aisling found it amusing to watch, unlike Moira who was appalled by anyone over the age of thirty engaging in flirtatious banter. 'Sure, it'd be like Mammy trying to have her way with him so it would,' she'd shuddered. 'Bronagh needs to find a man her own age. I might suggest she joins lawn bowls, it's a sea of silver heads.' Moira's tongue could clip a hedge at times, but she did make her laugh. Aisling had told her that Bronagh was only in her mid-fifties and that lawn bowls was having a resurgence with the younger generation to which she'd replied tongue firmly in cheek, 'it would be right up Bronagh's alley then.'

'I will,' Aisling tossed back over her shoulder now as she turned the brass knob and opened the door. She shut it behind her before the wind got a chance to catch it. One of the familiar Hop-on Hop-off red Dublin tour buses whooshed past. There was a handful of hardy tourists huddled upstairs, cameras at the ready as they braved the elements. She paused to gaze wistfully across the road to the tree-lined park. It wouldn't be long before the leaves began to fall. When was the last time she'd taken a book and stretched out on the grass on the Green? She'd missed the boat there this year, it was too cold to do so now.

She used to love losing herself in a good story. She'd let the world pass her by making the most of the sunshine like any good Irish woman would—turning a blind eye to the luminous white, male chests on display. Aisling knew the answer to her question. The last time she'd picked up a book and whiled away a leisurely few hours on the Green lost in someone else's story was when she'd come home to O'Mara's on her holidays. This was an anomaly given her job had always felt like one big holiday to her.

Back then, Dad had been well, and Mammy would shoo her away once she'd helped out with the breakfast telling her, 'Look you're due a break Aisling, go read your book.' She'd shake her head, 'How I wound up with such a bookworm is beyond me. You've never been any different though—always a dreamer. Right from when you were little your nose was buried in some book or other.'

It was true. She'd once hidden in the old dumb waiter with a torch in order to escape her chores—that's how desperate she'd been to finish whatever it was she'd been reading at the time!

Those were happy days, before Dad got sick and she'd come home for good. She'd stopped reading then, and there'd been no time for lazy afternoons laying on a grassy sunlit patch on the Green because Mammy's time had been sucked up taking care of Dad, and she'd needed all Aisling's help.

There was only one person to blame for her lack of work/ life balance this last year though. Well two, herself and Marcus. Mammy and her sisters were right when they said she wanted to be busy. It was her choice to throw herself into the routine of the guesthouse's daily tasks. She did so to avoid thinking. It hadn't worked of course. You couldn't bury your hurts.

The breeze was arctic, and she shivered before deciding if she walked briskly enough, she'd soon warm up. She set off following the Green around to Baggot Street. She was oblivious to the admiring glances from the women she passed who'd love to be able to stride along like Aisling O'Mara could in her blue patent leather high heels.

# Chapter 7

Aisling had always felt the tie to O'Mara's more keenly than her siblings. It was funny then that she'd been the first to leave it. She'd needed to get away after college, make a fresh start somewhere else.

She continued on her way dodging a young man whose nose was buried in a guidebook. His backpack was so big it made her think of a tortoise with a shell on its back. For a moment she felt a pang, envying his freedom.

As a child, it had been her, in between frantically turning the pages of a book who'd followed their mammy and dad as they went about their daily routine. She was eager to learn the ropes of running the popular guest house. She figured it was her love of stories that made her feel so strongly about O'Mara's. The old manor house abounded with them thanks to their guests. All of whom came from different walks of life and had different tales to tell as to their reasons for coming to stay. She'd felt, and still did for that matter, such a sense of pride that the house had been in their family for so many generations.

Aisling was lost in her thoughts as she reached the busy intersection and joined the cluster of people all waiting to cross. If she hadn't come home, then she wouldn't have met Marcus and put old ghosts to rest. Was it better to have loved and lost as the old saying went, than to never have loved at all? She'd loved twice, and she didn't know the answer. As her eyes alighted on Boots her deep thoughts were diverted as she remembered she was currently using her finger to gouge out what was left in her lipstick. She'd pop in now and buy a new one—and that was when she saw him.

# Chapter 8

Oh, Jaysus, it was Marcus; she was sure of it! It was as though just by thinking of him she'd conjured him up. What was he doing in Dublin? He was supposed to be miles away from her in Cork—not waiting at the lights to cross Baggot Street. She must be seeing things. When he'd first left, she used to think she saw him all the time. There'd been times she'd thought she really was going around the twist seeing these Marcus look-alikes everywhere. The mind can play funny tricks, and that was what it must be doing now.

Aisling peered around the burly man she was standing behind, but a bus rumbled past obscuring her view. It had only been a glimpse; maybe it wasn't him. She was having a Marcus-look-alike relapse that's all. She'd close her eyes for a tick and when she opened them again, she'd realise it was a stranger who had a similar look about him. It was her sub-conscious telling her to stop poring over his letters and move on.

She squeezed her eyes shut and then opening them peeped around the burly man again. *Feck, feck, feck.* It was definitely him; he was wearing the Oasis shirt she'd bought for him from their concert under his jacket. It was the most rock 'n' roll he ever got wearing that shirt. She felt herself spiral into fight-or-flight mode as her senses went into overdrive. Her heart began pounding and her skin prickled with cold, clammy sweat. What should she do? She'd never been much of a fighter and instinctively she wanted to run. To turn and run as fast as she could, back to the guesthouse, locking the door behind her in order to keep the big bad wolf out.

Marcus would see her if she made a holy show of herself by sprinting down St Stephen's Green. He hadn't spotted her yet. She was sure of it and, without thinking it through, Aisling veered off to her right. She kept her head lowered as she ducked and dived her way down the road heading into the sanctuary of O'Brien's sandwich bar.

The lunchtime queue was stretching long but thankfully hadn't reached the door, and she tagged onto the end of it behind two girls in office wear. The mundaneness of their conversation, what would have more calories a chicken Caesar wrap or a tuna melt? helped her to breathe and focus her thoughts. He must have been going to see her at the guesthouse. There was no other reason for him to be on fecking Baggot Street, for feck's sake! *Calm down, Aisling.*

She should have replied to his stupid letters and told him there wasn't a hope in hell of them getting back together. Not after what he'd done. She hadn't though, she'd let them pile up. Locking them away in the bureau drawer to pull out and angst over when no one was around, and now he was fecking well here.

She'd have to face the music sometime. She couldn't not go home. Besides, a spark of anger flared, why should she feel like she had to go into hiding because he'd decided he'd made a mistake? Look at her now for feck's sake. Swearing her head off, albeit silently, but if Mammy could hear her, she'd be threatening to wash her mouth out and she was hiding in a fecking sandwich shop!

She shouldn't allow him to affect her like this. She should have brazened it out, greeted him coolly, and made him feel foolish for wasting his time coming back to Dublin. Now the shock was wearing off, she mulled the situation over. Perhaps it was a good thing him coming to see her. If she talked to him face-to-face it might give her closure, and she'd finally stop having nightmares about white dresses with bodices of Irish lace and people staring at her sympathetically before whispering about her behind her back.

The queue shuffled forward. It was all well and good being brave and having bold thoughts of bringing her ex-fiancé down a peg or two as she hid in O'Brien's. How strong she'd be when they *did* meet was an entirely different matter altogether. His very presence had always affected her, given her a thrill each time she saw him.

She had no intention of ordering a sandwich of any description so excusing herself she pushed past the people who'd lined up behind her and ventured back out to the street. The coast was clear, so she continued down the road. Despite no sign of him, she was relieved when she spied the brass nameplate, Quinn's Bistro arching over the doorway of the white-washed, ground-floor restaurant.

There was a gorgeous profusion of pansies decorating the windows either side of the entrance and she knew credit for the beautiful floral displays didn't lie with Quinn. The hanging baskets overflowing with vibrant, pink and purple lobelia were lovingly tended by his maître d', Alasdair. He'd told her when she'd complimented him on his green fingers that he'd been head gardener for the lord and lady of a great house in a previous life.

A dose of Alasdair would take her mind off Marcus. He was one of a kind, with his flamboyant style and insistence on sharing the details of his past lives with anybody who cared, or didn't care for that matter, to listen. He was also, Quinn said, fabulous at his job. The punters loved him even if he had been a Viking warrior back in the days when they'd plundered Dublin!

She paused to eye the blackboard outside, liking the sound of slow cooked beef and Guinness stew. Her mouth watered, despite the fright she'd just had as her gaze darted down the handwritten menu, settling on a Baileys Irish cheesecake for dessert. She'd always loved her food and been prone to comfort eating. She was the girl who would get caught with her fingers raking through a tub of ice cream after a teenage drama. When Dad had been sick, she'd piled on the pounds. Then when he'd passed, she'd lost all interest in food despite Quinn's best efforts to keep her fed. He'd been such a good friend to her, to all the family. She'd lost her appetite when Marcus left too. Quinn had been a steady shoulder then as well.

She'd gotten her appetite back eventually, and sometimes comfort eating was the order of the day. She'd take Quinn up on his offer of dinner on the house. She needed a heart-to-heart with Leila. Her pragmatic friend would tell her what she should do where Marcus fecking coward McDonagh was concerned. Besides, it had been too long since they'd last caught up.

The cheery red door to the bistro opened, emitting a burst of noisy chatter from inside. A girl around Moira's age, in a skirt so tight it would surely split if she bent over, tottered out. An older man in a well-cut suit, looking very pleased with himself, followed behind her. There was a furtiveness about them and Aisling watched them from under her lashes. She'd put money on wandering hands under the table as they waited for their Quinn's burger and bangers 'n' mash. She found herself composing one of her letters. The image of a world-weary, middle-aged woman who'd been let down by her husband sprang to mind. She was sitting at her kitchen table, pen poised over a writing pad.

*Dear Aisling,*

*My husband often takes his young secretary out for lunch. He says it's thanking her for being so efficient. He comes home smelling of perfume and bangers 'n' mash. It's a cliché, but I think they're having an affair. What should I do? Confront him about my suspicions or continue to bury my head in the sand?*

*Yours faithfully,*

*Wronged Woman*

God, Mammy always said her talents were wasted—*with your imagination, Aisling, and your love of books,* she'd say, *you should have been a writer. Sure, look at the success that Keyes woman is having.* She also said she should have been on the stage when she had one of her dramatic outbursts. She said it quite a lot come to think of it. Instead, she'd qualified with a much more practical Diploma in Tourism. It didn't stop her imagination running riot though and it was getting out of hand. She was seeing philanderers everywhere these days. These two had probably had a perfectly innocent business luncheon. She changed her mind a beat later as the man planted his hand firmly on the girl's derrière. *Dirty old sod.*

Shaking her head, she pushed open the bistro door and stepped inside the humming interior. She loved Quinn's with its exposed bricks and low timber beams. The atmosphere was always inviting, especially come winter when the log fire was roaring. What she loved most of all though was the aroma of garlic and onions that hung in the air. It called to her to take a load off and make herself at home.

Alasdair looked up from where he was flicking through the reservation book. 'Aisling O'Mara, my Dublin Rose! My one true love.' He clapped his hands like a small child having been told they were going to McDonald's for dinner, before mincing toward her. He lunged at her cheeks, kissing the left then the right side, before resting his hands on either side of her shoulders. 'You know, ours was the greatest love affair of all.'

This was what she needed, Aisling smiled at him, playing along with the banter.

'I was a penniless artist, you were the beautiful daughter of wealthy parents. We met on an epic voyage at sea but sadly it ended in tragedy.' His hand fluttered to his chest.

'Hmm, tell me, Alasdair, did your name happen to be Jack and mine Rose?'

'You feel the connection too.'

'I saw Titanic twice.' She grinned. He was a tonic. 'Now then, Jack, would you have a table for four available for tonight at five-thirty? It's short notice but our guests asked me for a dinner recommendation at breakfast this morning, and you know Quinn's is always my first port of call.'

'For which we are eternally grateful, and if there is no room ma petite fleur, we will make room.'

'Thank you. Oh, and I need some brochures while I'm here too; we've nearly run out.'

His dark head bobbed beneath the counter and Aisling waited while he crouched down to peer inside the cupboard under the cash register. He popped back up like a jack-in-the-box with a stack of pamphlets for her as the phone began to trill and the door to the street opened.

'Sorry, Alasdair, silly time to call in. You answer that, and I'll go say a quick hello to Quinn.'

He blew her a kiss before calling out a 'Hello, darlings, I'll be with you in two ticks,' to the man and woman who'd just walked in.

Aisling left him to multi-task with the phone and customers as she weaved her way around the tables. She smiled a hello at Paula, the waitress, whose notepad was in hand as she made her way over to a table full of boisterous women. Seeing them all laughing, having a great craic, reinforced Aisling's resolve to make a date with Leila the moment she got home. She crossed her fingers, hopefully Marcus would be long gone when she got back, for today at least.

# Chapter 9

Aisling pushed open the swinging doors and was assailed with a deliciously rich waft of meats and vegetables simmering away inside the frenetic kitchen. Quinn was over by the gas hobs, his head down in conversation with the sous-chef as they discussed whatever it was bubbling in one of the many pots being tended to. His blond hair was just visible beneath his hat. The sous-chef spotted her first, giving Quinn a nudge.

His face she saw was flushed from the steam and he needed a shave, which she'd be sure to tell him, but it was nice that his blue eyes lit up at the sight of her. 'Aisling! How's the form?' He wiped his hands on his chequered pants before striding over to wrap her in a hello hug. She hugged him back just as warmly.

'Grand,' she lied. 'It's a bad time to call I know, right on lunchtime. I don't know what I was thinking other than I fancied a bit of air. I had to make a reservation for some guests and pick up more of these so that's my excuse.' She held up the pamphlets. She wouldn't mention having seen Marcus from afar less than fifteen minutes ago. She knew Quinn's opinion of him and it wasn't high. Come to think of it, it hadn't exactly been glowing before Marcus had jilted her. The feeling between the two men was mutual and she'd never figured out why. Neither had said anything but she could tell by their macho posturing when they were in one another's company.

'How's your mam getting on?' she asked. Mrs Doherty had suffered a stroke a month back. Aisling had dropped a bunch of flowers around a few weeks ago. It had been a shock to see her looking frail and well, old, especially when she'd always been so sprightly. Aisling hoped given time, she would get back to how she was before it happened.

He rubbed at the stubble on his chin. 'Alright. She's definitely slowed down, and she gets frustrated you know, having to rely on me or Dad to take her everywhere. The doctor's not given her the all clear to drive yet.'

'Give her my love, won't you?'

'I will do. And what about your mam—is she enjoying being by the sea?'

It was a sign they were getting older Aisling thought, them asking after each other's

mammy's like so. There was a time—it didn't seem all that long ago—they'd have been moaning how banjaxed they were after Thursday night's rave up.

'Ah, she loves it, Quinn. I swear everything in her wardrobe is nautical stripes these days, and she's even taken to wearing boat shoes. I never thought I'd see my mammy in flats, but fair play to her, she'd look a bit odd in her striped tops and white pants with a pair like this on her feet.' She gestured to her impractical footwear.

'The thing is she's never even been on a boat other than the Dún Laoghaire to Holyhead ferry. Mind you I've heard her making noises about sailing lessons so, it's only a matter of time.' Aisling shook her head. 'She's gone a bit mad taking up art classes and joining everything from the golf club to bowls. Oh, and she's on about the yacht club too now. She's managed to slot Moira and me into her busy calendar for lunch tomorrow.'

Quinn smiled gently. 'She's a good woman your mam, and to be fair now she nursed your poor dad until the end. Losing someone you expected to spend your retirement with would change your perspective on things. I expect she needs to keep herself busy.'

'When did you get so wise?' Aisling's eyes prickled unexpectedly with tears and she blinked them away. She didn't want to stand here snivelling in Quinn's busy kitchen but Dad's death, even though it had been a blessed relief when the time came, was still raw and the pain snuck up on her when she least expected it. For Mammy to have grabbed life by the horns with quite as much vigour as she had was a shock too. She'd no desire to spend the rest of her days mouldering in O'Mara's with her memories she'd said. Then she'd signed on the dotted line for a modern two-bedroom apartment with views out over Howth Harbour.

'I don't know about wise,' Quinn said, his eyes flicking over to the kitchen hand, who was taking advantage of his boss being occupied to check his mobile phone instead of cracking on with the chopping of vegetables. 'Observant maybe.'

'You're that alright, you never did miss much. Remember when you told me that Diarmud and Orla from our old college gang had the hots for each other?'

He nodded.

'And I said you needed your eyes checking because Orla fancied Diarmud about as much as I liked Bono.' Aisling could never understand what all the fuss was about where the Irish rocker was concerned. It was something she'd been verbal about after a few pints of Guinness from time to time.

'And now they're married.'

'With four children, no less.'

They both laughed.

Paula pushed past, calling out an order.

'Does your dinner on the house offer still stand? Because I'm due to catch up with Leila and I was eyeing the slow cooked Guinness and beef stew on the board out the front before I came in.'

'Of course! Let me know a time, and I'll make sure we've got a table.'

'Thanks, Quinn, and you'll join I us I hope,' she said, before adding, 'It'd be good to sit down and have a proper natter. Anyway, I'll leave you to it.'

'I'd like that. It's been too long since we three had a catch up. It was good to see you, Aisling. Take care now. Remember me to your mam too.'

'And me to yours. Oh, and Quinn—,'

He raised a questioning eyebrow.

'Be sure and have a shave tonight won't you?'

'What? Are you not keen on my rugged Brad Pitt, Fight Club look? All the girls love him.'

'You're more a Ronan Keating type than Brad Pitt.'

'Ah well, the girls love him too.'

Aisling grinned, there was a time when she'd been smitten with Quinn Moran back in their college days. She still had a soft spot for him, it was something she'd learned to live with because he'd never looked at her in that way. She never let on how she felt for fear of ruining their friendship. Then she'd gone abroad for work needing to put some space between him and her mixed-up feelings. All of that was a lifetime ago, ancient history. 'Bronagh sends her best. And remember to shave!' She mimicked shaving her jawline before turning and exiting out the swinging doors.

Aisling waved goodbye to Alasdair. She had to laugh hearing him tell a snappily dressed customer that he was sure they'd met each other before when they'd both been gentry landowners in the seventeenth century.

~

Quinn watched Aisling leave, a wistful look on his face. Despite his swagger, there was only one girl he wanted to love him, but it had never occurred to her to look at him in that way. His love for Aisling had been a slow burn on his part. He'd been aware she was gorgeous but still their relationship had begun platonically with a friendship formed at college. They got around in the same group and all had a great craic together. Then the realisation had hit one night as they neared graduation, somewhere along the way his feelings had taken root and grown into something deeper.

It was a million little things, like the way she tossed her head back and laughed, the slight dimpling in her cheek when she smiled. The sparkle in her eyes when she told a story or the way she'd leap off her stool to do the actions whenever the Macarena came on.

He could have said something back then on one of their many nights out, but he was scared. If she didn't feel the same way, he'd lose her friendship because there'd be no going back to the way things were once he'd crossed that line. So he said nothing.

'Quinn, the water's boiling away on the potatoes.'

He jerked out of his reverie and did what he always did after he'd seen Aisling, threw himself back into his work.

# Chapter 10

Aisling dragged her heels all the way up St Stephen's Green, feeling like Mr Fox as she furtively scanned the faces heading towards her. All three storeys of O'Mara's loomed over her and she was relieved to have reached the guest house with no sighting of Marcus. She stood outside staring at the window box with its profusion of purple and yellow pansies, debating whether she should try to sneak a peek in through the windows. The problem was solved for her when the door opened and Mr Peterson, camera in hand appeared. 'I forgot this,' he said in his posh Queen's English, as he held the door for her. She had no choice but to venture inside.

'Thank you,' she said. 'You and Mrs Peterson be sure to have a lovely afternoon.'

'We will, thank you, dear.'

'There you are!' Bronagh's jet black head with its telltale zebra stripe at the roots bobbed up from behind the computer, her brown eyes, rimmed with a generous application of black liner, were ginormous and round. 'You'll never guess who had the brass neck to bowl in here while you were out.'

'Let me take a wild stab in the dark. Marcus?'

Bronagh's eyes shrank back to their normal size. 'Have you seen him then?'

'No. Well yes, but from a safe distance and he didn't see me. He was crossing Baggot Street, so I guessed this was where he was heading. I went and hid in O'Brien's.'

'If I'd known you were ducking in there, I would have got you to pick me up one of their chicken wraps, they're lovely.' She looked down at the plate next to the keyboard on which a sad looking sandwich triangle sat. 'I don't even like tomato, but its low calorie.'

'Bronagh, food was the last thing on my mind. What did you say to him?'

'I told him you'd gone to live in an ashram in India.'

'You didn't?'

'I'd have liked to. I'd have liked to tell him to feck off too, excuse my French but, after what he did—'

'Bronagh, just tell me what you said.'

She picked up her sandwich. 'I told him you were out doing errands and wouldn't be back in until later. And, I might have told him you were out tonight too. I didn't want him thinking you spend your nights sitting up there,' she pointed to the ceiling, 'pining for him.'

'I don't.' She did. 'But thanks.' She couldn't stop herself asking, 'How did he seem?'

'Not his usual cock o' the walk self.' Her eyes narrowed. 'Aisling do not feel sorry for the man. He doesn't deserve it.'

'I wasn't.' That much was true at least. 'I'm going to head upstairs for a bit, make a few phone calls while it's quiet. I'll leave you to your tomato sandwich.'

Bronagh muttered something about soggy bread and feckless men under her breath as Aisling powered up the stairs. She'd phone Leila now while she was on her mind. Besides, she needed to offload her news on someone who'd helped pick up the pieces after he left.

~

'Good afternoon, Love Leila Bridal Planning, Leila speaking.'

'Leila it's me.'

'Who? I don't recognise that voice?'

'Don't be an eejit. I know it's been a while. I just saw Marcus.'

'No!'

'Yes.'

'Feck.'

'Exactly.'

'He looked the same. I was hoping he might have turned into a short fat garden gnome but he hasn't.' Aisling curled up in her favourite chair. It was dappled with pools of sunlight from the window behind it and she filled her friend in on her last few hours.

'Think Bono, Ash. I can't believe the nerve of the man. Why's he back now?'

'Well, there's something I haven't told you. I haven't told anybody. He's been writing to me.'

'Aisling. You're a soft touch so you are. I hope you haven't replied.'

'No, but that's the thing. If I had, I mean if I'd spelled it out there wasn't going to be a second chance he might have stayed in Cork. Oh, Leila, what am I going to do? I don't trust myself to be around him. I'll either rage at him, or sob and I don't know what would be worse.'

'Definitely the sobbing. Run with the rage. Tell him the truth, Ash, tell him how much he hurt you, how he broke your trust and it can't be fixed.' Her friend's tone was steely.

But could it? Aisling wondered. What if he meant what he'd been saying in his letters? What if she were to forgive him and try again?

'Look, I'm sorry, Ash, but I have to go, I've a bridezilla to meet in fifteen minutes and she's already teetering on the edge. She went overboard with the teeth whitening and her poor fiancé is going to have to wear sunglasses on their big day.'

'Tell her to drink lots of coffee and red wine between now and then.'

They both sniggered.

'Before you go, the other reason I rang was to invite you to dinner, on Quinn at Quinn's. When are you free?'

'As incredible as it might seem, my social calendar is surprisingly empty aside from attending other people's weddings. How about Sunday?'

'Seven?'

'See you then.'

Aisling hung up. The three bedroomed space, with its kitchen and a large living area had always seemed full to the brim when they were growing up, despite the generous proportions. Right now though it just seemed empty and full of echoes.

The apartment had once upon a time, in the Georgian's heyday, been the top floor servant quarters. The O'Mara's had been quite well-to-do back then, but those days were long gone and it was hard to imagine leading such a pampered life now. Aisling spied Moira's dressing gown. It was in a crumpled heap at the end of the sofa, her breakfast bowl and coffee mug abandoned on the coffee table. It was a lifestyle her sister, with her penchant for not picking up after herself, would adapt well to.

It had been her grandparents who'd converted the many rooms into a guest house. Hard times had hit, and it was the only way to keep the grand old building in the family. When they'd died, it had passed down the line to her father, an only child, and he'd taken up the reins.

She was too small to remember a time when she hadn't called the manor house home. She loved it. The rooms possessed an olde-worlde charm with their myriad nooks and crannies. Even the dumb waiter was still in working order. It ran all the way from the basement kitchen to their apartment and had been a favourite hiding place as a child. Most of all though, she loved the view from their living room to the bustling street below and the peaceful Green beyond.

Her eyes settled on the bureau drawer and she unfurled herself from the chair feeling an almost magnetic pull toward it. She wandered over and retrieved the key, on automatic pilot as she unlocked the drawer. She stared at the bundle of letters for a moment before picking them up. Sitting down at the table, she opened the last one Marcus had sent her.

She knew the sentiments by heart, they all said variations of the same thing. He was sorry. He should never have left her. The biggest regret of his life was not having the courage to marry her but the biggest cliché of them all was Marcus had gotten cold feet.

Her eyes misted over as she read over the words she'd already read time and time again.

# Chapter 11
## One year earlier or thereabouts

'Breathe in, Aisling. I'm wondering if you should have gone for size twelve,' Leila said wriggling the zipper slowly up Aisling's back.

Aisling gulped in air and held her tummy in as tightly as she could. 'No, I've still got two weeks to lose a few pounds. I'll stop sniffing around Quinn's kitchen and I might try the soup diet. I like a bit of leek and potato soup.' She looked at her maid of honour. She was a picture in the soft blue, almost grey dress she'd picked out for her bridesmaids. The colour suited Leila's light blue eyes and blonde hair. It was down around her shoulders now but on the day, it would be worn up.

Moira, who'd wanted her, Leila, and Roisin to wear her favourite colour lilac was sitting in the chair in the corner of the expansive plush dressing room of Ivory Bridal Couture. She looked bored as she fiddled with her phone. She was always on the thing, thumb frantically pushing buttons. Aisling couldn't see the attraction of always being contactable and had not succumbed to a mobile phone. Meanwhile, Roisin, who'd carefully relayed her measurements over the phone was arriving in Dublin next week and would have her final fitting then. She'd wanted pink dresses, but Aisling had stuck to her guns because as soon as she'd laid eyes on the simple, blue silk cowl neck dress she'd fallen in love. Besides, the colour would look well on all three of them.

Leila moved Aisling's hair out the way as she finally wrested the zip into place. She stepped back to admire her friend's reflection in the big floor-to-ceiling mirror at the far end of the dressing room. 'There, now look at you. I think you're the most beautiful bride-to-be I've ever seen—and I've seen a few.'

'Even if I do need to lose a couple of pounds,' Aisling laughed. 'And besides, I think you might be a little biased.'

Moira piped up, 'Five pounds at least, Aisling, and if you're going to do the soup diet, I think they're supposed to be clear soups, not potato and cream based.'

Aisling poked her tongue out at her. She did have a point though, and Moira was in her good books for putting Mammy off. She'd not wanted her coming along with them to this their final fitting. Mammy meant well but Maureen O'Mara was a woman of many words. Which was a polite way of saying sometimes she had too much to say for herself.

She was bossy where her three girls were concerned. A tiger mama. She'd driven poor Roisin demented in the lead-up to her big day. When her sister had rung to congratulate Aisling on her engagement she'd added sagely, 'As your big sister who's been there and done that, Ash, I want you to promise me something.'

'What is it?' Aisling wasn't promising anything until she knew what she was in for.

'Trust me on this. Don't let Mammy come with you to choose your dress or to any of your fittings. Do you remember our holy communion?'

'How could I forget? Mammy turned into a monster. We had to have the biggest and best dresses. We looked like tiny versions of Princess Diana on her wedding day. Dad was going mad over the cost of it all. Who knew she was so competitive?'

'Exactly, she was terrible when you were seven years old and committing yourself to Christ, imagine what she'll be like now you're thirty-four marrying a flesh and blood man—*and* she had you pegged as being on the shelf. That's extra interfering points right there and it'll be worse for you now her time's her own. Mark my words, you give her an inch when it comes to your wedding, she'll have you in a frothy white monstrosity. If she'd had her way, I would have wound up wearing a blancmange. Jaysus, the row we had in Abigail's Brides to Be, I thought Abigail was going to bar the pair of us.'

She'd heeded Roisin's words of wisdom despite feeling a little mean at not including Mammy. To be fair though, she had plenty to keep her otherwise occupied. There was her plethora of social groups, and in her rare downtime she was throwing a lot of energy into her mother-of the-bride dress. She'd confided this was because she wasn't going to be outdone by Mrs McDonagh who, what with Marcus being an only child, was sure to go to town with her outfit. So with Moira's help, the first opportunity Mammy would have to see her in her dress was on the day itself.

Aisling felt a frisson of sadness as she turned to the left and then to the right. She'd wanted Dad to walk her down the aisle but instead his brother Cormac would do the honours. It still took her by surprise from time to time that Dad was no longer with them. It was also hard to believe if she hadn't come back to Dublin to take over O'Mara's she'd never have met Marcus.

Perhaps it was fate's way of softening the blow of losing her father. She blinked back the sudden smarting of tears and turned
her mind to the guesthouse for a second. Bronagh would have
everything under control and Nina was perfectly able to manage the quieter evenings. She was grateful to the two women,
their reliability and capability left her free to concentrate on
this, admiring her dress.

She'd fallen in love with it the moment Niamh, Ivory Couture's owner, had pulled it from the rack. The mermaid trumpet
style with its overlay of white Irish lace was not what she'd gone
for initially. When she'd daydreamed of her big day, she was always in something princess-like with a tiara, there was always a
tiara. Niamh's well-practised eye had taken in Aisling's curves
however and gently steered her away from her first choice.

She was so glad she had because Roisin's terminology of
looking like a blancmange sprang to mind now. This mermaid
trumpet gown was the most gorgeous dress she'd ever worn. It
even eclipsed her love for the Prada satin pumps she'd picked
out to wear with it. This was her Cinderella dress and it em-
braced her hourglass form. Even if she didn't manage to lose
those pesky few pounds, she'd be fine on the day so long as she
didn't breathe or sit down!

Niamh popped her head in and tweaked the bodice of Aisling's dress, so she wasn't revealing quite so much cleavage. She
turned her attention to Moira's hem, gesturing for her to stand.
Her sister obliged, and a debate raged as to whether it might
need to be taken up half an inch. Moira convinced her to leave
it as it was by telling her she planned on wearing heels higher
than the ones she presently had on so the length wouldn't be an
issue.

All the O'Mara women were short, the height gene had gone directly from Dad to Patrick. As such Maureen, Roisin, Aisling, and Moira all insisted on wear ankle breaking heels to even up the odds.

Once Niamh had finished her final titivations, the girls got changed back into their civvies. Leila, pulling on her jeans, suggested a drink on the way home to run through the day itself one last time. Her wedding planning service was her gift to Aisling and one for which she was grateful. There was nobody else she would have trusted to help her pull off the most important day of her life. Certainly not her Mammy! Moira bowed out having already made plans to catch up with her friends at a pub where a new band they'd heard good things about was playing. So Aisling and Leila, arm in arm, made their way down busy O'Connell Street with its Friday night vibe in full swing as people finished work for the week.

'The Gresham? We'll be able to hear ourselves think in there,' Leila suggested, and Aisling agreed.

They found a table in the civilised Writer's Lounge and sat opposite one another chatting until their drinks arrived. A low-calorie vodka soda for Aisling and a pint of Guinness for Leila. She'd ordered a honey glazed ham sandwich too, and Aisling watched on enviously as she scoffed it down. Leila had hollow legs and never gained a pound. She also never stopped, she was one hundred miles an hour darting here, there, and everywhere as she made sure her clients had the best day of their lives.

Aisling was hardly sedentary but no matter how many times she trooped up and down the flights of stairs at home, she always seemed to hold on to an extra few pounds. They clung to her rather like a toxic friend she couldn't get rid of. She dabbed at the crumbs left on Leila's plate and popped her finger in her mouth.

Leila produced the folder she'd compiled for Aisling and Marcus's nuptials and Aisling pored over the booklet for Lisnavagh Castle. The princess dress might have gone, but the castle hadn't, and she was having a tiara, that went without saying. Lisnavagh Castle, nestled against the lush green and gold countryside of Wicklow, was dreamy. It was the stuff of fairy tales. She flicked through the glossy pages eagerly, sighing over the picturesque setting. The sun would shine on her day, she was sure of it, just like it was in the pictures she was gazing at.

Mammy had suggested having the reception at O'Mara's like Roisin had. Their guesthouse had done her sister proud on the day, but Aisling lived and worked there, she didn't want to hold her wedding there too. Marcus who would be moving in after their Maldives honeymoon agreed with her. At least he hadn't disagreed when she'd stated that as they were paying for the wedding themselves, they should be able to hold it where they wanted. She hadn't felt the least bit guilty booking the extravagant venue. She only planned on doing this once, and she wanted it to be perfect.

Leila and Aisling whiled away a companionable hour discussing seating arrangements. The hot topic; where to put her dad's bite of a sister Aunt Delia? 'I think we should sit her next to Great Aunt Maggie, she's a bit doolally so Aunt Delia's moaning about the soup not having enough salt or the duck skin not being crispy enough won't faze her.' Aisling announced pleased with her solution.

Aisling had a slight flush to her cheeks by the time they left the bar and made their way home. It was partly due to the vodka soda, but it was also excitement. She couldn't wait for the sixth of September when she would become Mrs Marcus Mc-Donagh. Leila walked with her across O'Connell Bridge before hugging her goodbye. She would catch the DART from Tara Station to her Blackrock home. The evening was warm despite it officially being autumn now, and the streets around Grafton Street were buzzing with early revellers. The joviality was infectious and Aisling had a spring in her step. She paused to watch a young violinist playing near Marks & Spencer, fishing around inside her purse for some coins to throw him.

She'd have liked to learn to play an instrument. Mammy had sent her off to piano lessons after school but like her singing, she'd no natural aptitude for it. She could, however, dance and standing there caught up in the music she lost herself in memories recalling how she'd first crossed paths with Marcus.

~

Aisling had been installed back in her old room at O'Mara's—which she thankfully now had to herself—for two weeks when she met the man she was going to marry. Moira had commandeered what had been Mammy and Dad's bedroom, the largest of the three, and had already managed to make it look as though some sort of clothes bomb had detonated in there.

It was unsettling being home. O'Mara's felt different without Mammy and Dad buzzing about the place. It was hard to accept that Dad, their lovely, calm, steady father had passed. That he wasn't here filling the spaces, a strong shoulder always there for them all to lean on.

Aisling didn't like to dwell on the empty spot he'd left behind. It was like poking at the pain with a lance. It would ooze fresh and raw with each prod. It was strange too accepting this new Mammy, a mam without Dad at her side tempering her. The life Aisling had known since gaining her diploma, of flitting from one glorious sunshine destination to another, already seemed a distant memory.

She loved the city she'd been born in, but she hadn't planned on coming back, not for a while at any rate. Hania, where she'd been managing a resort in need of being brought up to speed alongside its competitors, had been a little piece of paradise. The beautiful old town with its brilliant colours and that sky! It melded with the sea in a never-ending panorama of blue.

That was her old life she told herself. It had never been her real life she realised now. Merely a stopgap. There would have come a time when all that globetrotting had gotten tiresome, it was just the decision to come home had been made sooner than she'd planned. It didn't matter how she tried to convince herself coming home was inevitable though, settling back in was easier said than done.

Thinking back on it the company she worked for had been generous, more than generous really. They'd allowed her an extended period off to come home and help when Dad's illness was too much for Mammy to cope with. It had helped they were heading into the quiet shoulder season and she would soon have found herself winging her way to a busier climate anyway—job done. She supposed in a way the timing had been convenient for them.

She'd arranged to stay on in Dublin for a week longer following Dad's funeral. It had been, as per his wishes, a simple affair. For once Mammy had not tried to go bigger and better, she'd honoured his wishes. It was two days later when Maureen O'Mara had thrown the spanner in the works with her announcement that she would not be staying on at the guesthouse without her husband.

They were all there gathered around the dining table, Patrick, Roisin, Moira, and herself—oh and Colin the Arse had squeezed himself in beside his wife. It was like a scene from a film where the wizened lawyer reads the patriarch's last will and testament. Only there was no lawyer and no will, just Mammy, and she was firm and resolute in her decision. She claimed it wasn't rash, she'd had plenty of time to mull over her future while sitting at Dad's bedside these last few months. They'd discussed it while he was still well enough, she told them. Together they'd amassed a tidy sum over the years, all put away for a rainy day. Now that rainy day had come, and she wanted out.

The cards were laid on the table. Mammy refused to entertain the idea of a stranger managing the place, her argument being O'Mara's had always been a family business. She'd rather sell and divvy up the proceeds than trust their family name to a stranger. If however, one of her children wished to take over the day-to-day running of the guesthouse, it would stay in the family. This was, of course, the preferable option, although she understood that while building O'Mara's into what it was today had been her and Dad's dream, it might not necessarily be theirs.

Children had a right to follow their own dreams, she proclaimed. It would be sad to sell, to lose the family connection with the building but when it came down to it O'Mara's was just a building after all. They were not to feel beholden she said. Dad had made his peace with whatever choices were made once he'd gone.

Moira was far too flighty for the role and Mammy had enough trouble without adding her to the list. Roisin had stayed out of the negotiations not offering an opinion on what should happen with the family business one way or the other—unlike her husband. Her life was in London with the Arse and with little Noah. Her feisty wilful big sister seemed to have morphed into a meek and moany sort since she'd gotten married. Mind you, he was a bossy so-and-so, her brother-in-law. He'd stamp all over single-mindedness. She supposed her sister found it easier to acquiesce than to rock the boat. Which left Patrick.

Her brother referred to himself as an entrepreneur. A job description, from what Aisling could see, on a par with being a Director of Housekeeping. It too entailed doing a lot of not very much at all. He spent his time swanning around the city in a flashy car and in his world, it was important to be seen at the best restaurants and bars on offer. Somehow though he seemed to make shed loads of money.

Aisling's blood had boiled as she spied the predatory gleam in Patrick's eyes. He looked positively gleeful at the thought of all that freed up equity if the building were sold. Her gaze had swung in Colin the Arse's direction and she'd seen the greedy glimmer in his eyes too. That same afternoon once everybody had dispersed to mull over what had been said Aisling had taken herself quietly off. The decision had been an easy one, she telephoned her employers to thank them for their generosity and kindness toward her during her father's illness. She had however decided she was needed permanently at home. She wouldn't be coming back.

Thank goodness for Leila and Quinn. She'd have been lost without their friendship and support. The years away had given her perspective on those mixed-up feelings she had for Quinn. They were friends—it was all they'd ever be, and it would have to be enough. So she'd picked up with her two old pals as though she'd only seen them yesterday.

It was Leila who'd suggested they head along and check out Monday night salsa dance classes. It would do them all good to stretch their cultural boundaries, she said. And that's where she'd met Marcus.

# Chapter 12

To learn Latin American dance was not something Aisling had ever thought about doing, but it could be fun. The exercise would be good too, a much more fun way of keeping fit than pounding it out at a gym. Not that she had any intention of doing that! Salsa could be something positive that would take her away from her grief and O'Mara's for a few hours at least.

'C'mon, Ash it will be a good craic so it will,' Leila pressured. 'And Quinn won't come unless you do; he said he's two left feet and he's only prepared to humiliate himself if you are too. Say you'll give it a go.'

'But what would I wear?'

'Something comfortable and practical, but sexy and evocative at the same time—you know, like Latin music. Then again, you don't want to distract your partner by wearing something too sexy, he might be so busy staring down your top he stamps on your foot or something.'

'Not if I'm partnering with Quinn, he'd be oblivious if I were dancing the tango topless, and that really didn't help, Leila.'

Leila giggled. 'I just imagined him in tight black trousers shaking a castanet and wiggling his hips around like yer man Ricky Martin. And who said he's going to be your partner, I'm the one trying to convince him to come.'

'Ah, but he won't come unless I agree to go too.'

'Fair play. I hope you're coordinated. Whoever you wind up partnering with could lose a toe with one of your stiletto heels.'

'Shake your bon-bon!' Aisling sang, and she and Leila collapsed in a fit of snorting giggles. When they'd sobered, Leila announced, 'I'm going to get in the swing of it by wearing a fitted black dress and I might put a rose behind my ear.'

'You're thinking of the tango, not salsa you eejit.'

'Oh, so I am. Ah well, we'll figure it out,' she laughed.

'Looks like I'm going to be learning salsa. You'd better tell Quinn there's no getting out of it now!'

~

The classes were held in a dance studio hidden away above a cluster of shops on Dame Street. The businesses were all closed for the day by the time Aisling, Leila, and Quinn, who'd been dragging his heels all the way there, arrived at the address. They opened the door with the name plate that said they had come to the right place, Lozano's Dance Studio and Leila led the way up the stairs. Aisling brought up the rear making sure Quinn, who thankfully had opted for sweat pants, not tight trousers, and was not carrying a castanet so far as she could tell, didn't try to make a getaway.

A light shone under the double doors at the top of the landing. They could hear a fast Latin beat reverberating as they hovered for a moment. They looked from one to the other, uncertain as to whether they should knock or barrel straight in. Leila opted to be bold and pushed open the doors. The trio blinked as they found themselves in a brightly lit studio. There was a vast polished parquet dance floor, a mirrored floor to ceiling wall and on the side of the room with the windows over-looking Dame Street below, a stretch of bar.

Aisling's eyes alighted on a woman who looked like she should be at a ballet class. She was dressed in a leotard and tights, with a wraparound skirt worn over, her right leg stretched out along the bar as she warmed up. *Just how physical was this going to be?* she wondered, eyeing the rest of her class-mates; they were a mixed bag.

A group of girls around Moira's age were giggling in the far corner aware they were being eyed by the cluster of twenty-something young men. There were two middle-aged couples in deep conversation, here to spice up their marriages, perhaps. A younger couple had their heads bent together and she looked as though she was giving him a talking to. Aisling could see the light catching the sparkly diamond on the girl's finger as she prodded him in the chest and she automatically penned one of her imaginary letters.

*Dear Aisling,*

*My fiancé and I are getting married in two months. I want us to perform salsa at the reception to entertain our guests, instead of a boring traditional first dance. I've enrolled us in lessons and he is making the biggest song and dance about going. If he can't do something simple like learn a few new dance steps for me, how does that bode for our married life together?*

*Yours faithfully,*

*Getting Cold Feet*

~

A couple who looked to be around Mammy's age were tak-ing a twirl on the floor at the far end of the studio. She watched them for a beat, their ease with each other giving away the fact they'd danced like this in their youth. It made her think how unfair it was Mammy and Dad had been robbed of the chance to while away their golden retirement years together learning to salsa. Mind you, Moira would have had something to say about her parents gyrating against one another on a dance floor. The thought of the look on her face were she here now made her smile and chased off the sad thoughts.

She sensed Quinn tense next to her and reached over and squeezed his hand. 'It will be gas, you'll see.'

She refrained from telling him Moira had erupted in laughter upon hearing her sister's plans for the next six Wednesday nights. 'Three sad-arsed thirty-plus singletons learning salsa together!' she'd shrieked. Aisling had flicked a pea from her plate across the table at her. She might be a thirty-something, but she could be just as childish as her sister. Besides, there was nothing sad-arsed about it. The three of them had been too busy building their careers to devote time to serious relationships. She said this to her sister who looked unimpressed as she picked up the pea that had just landed on her lap.

They'd all taken different paths upon leaving college. Quinn had opted to serve under a demanding Michelin starred chef at a top London eatery, learning his trade from the bottom up. He'd come back to Dublin five years ago, having decided he was ready to open his own restaurant. Leila meanwhile had worked as a bridal designer's assistant for one of Dublin's leading lights in the industry until she decided the time had come to build her own business. Aisling had taken to travel like a baby bird discovering its wings. She'd worked at resorts in the Whitsunday's in Australia, then Fiji, Hawaii, the Seychelles, and her last position in Crete.

They were all married to their jobs and had gotten very serious in their post-college years. You'd never believe the hijinks they used to get up to now. Yes, putting themselves outside of their comfort zone by doing something different like learning a Latin American dance would do them no harm whatsoever.

'It's a fecking meat market that's what it is,' Quinn muttered, his eyes moving toward the glamorous duo currently pressed together in the centre of the room.

'I think that's Maria and Antonio Lozano,' Leila whispered, her eyes wide. 'They're good, aren't they?'

Aisling nodded, watching them. They were so lithe, so graceful. And yes, okay, they did look as though they should get a room but wasn't that what this dance was all about? Shouldn't you feel as though you were watching something deeply intimate and sensual? She glanced down at her plain black skirt. She'd teemed it with a white t-shirt. She felt frumpy and short, despite her heels, compared to the elegant instructor in her daring red dress.

The skirt she'd chosen might be plain, but it did billow out satisfyingly when she twirled. She knew this from having practised in front of the mirror in her bedroom. At least her Louboutin's (knock-offs but nobody needs know) added a touch of glamour. Leila had opted for a simple green dress with a snipped in waist that for some reason made Aisling think of Tinkerbell.

The song wound down and those who weren't on the dance floor applauded those that were. Maria and Antonio bowed, well used to the admiring glances. Antonio in his accented English welcomed them all, introducing himself and his wife,

Maria, who both had Cuban ancestry. He explained the origins of the dance they'd come to learn.

Aisling hadn't known it had originated in Eastern Cuba. Nor had she known that the name salsa was a broad term for many forms of Latin American dance. They would be learning to a fast beat called the timba which had its roots in the Afro-Cuban community. 'Salsa,' Antonio stated passionately, 'connects you with others. It is sexy and energetic. We come together to be our true selves and to be in the moment. Salsa is magic.' He performed some fancy and fast footwork before grabbing Mrs Lozano and spinning her round.

'Jaysus, feck,' muttered Quinn.

Leila whispered to Aisling, 'Will we be doing that bottom wobbling thing they do, do you think?'

'It's called twerking.'

It was then that the door opened, and Marcus walked in.

# Chapter 13

'I'm Marcus. Hi.'

'Aisling,' she smiled as the music started and Maria Lozano began to shout instructions over the top of it.

'I'm going to apologise in advance for crunching your toes.'

'Apology accepted.'

'I'm only here because I'm best man at a wedding next month. The bridal party is doing a Latin American dance at the reception for some unfathomable reason. Apparently, I don't have a natural aptitude so the bride-to-be booked me a lesson,' Marcus said. 'And I feel ridiculous.' He was jiggling his hips in her direction at the instruction of Antonio Lozano.

Aisling grinned to herself glancing over at the couple who'd inspired her 'Dear Aisling' letter. They'd been at odds when they first arrived, but he was looking even less impressed now. It didn't look like he had a natural aptitude for hip swivelling either. She hoped they made it down the aisle. It must be a new trend she decided—salsa dancing at weddings—and she made a mental note to ask Leila later. 'You're not alone, feeling ridiculous I mean,' she laughed turning her attention back to Marcus and quickly straightening her face upon receiving a glare from Mrs Lozano.

Salsa was not just magic, apparently it was a serious business too, or at least learning the basic steps was. This sexy man thrusting himself awkwardly at her could pass for a Latino she thought. Her pupils had dilated the moment he'd walked into the room apologising for being late. Leila had elbowed her, telling her to close her mouth, which she did. She'd already taken stock of his dark hair and serious eyes as they connected with hers.

He'd come to stand next to her and so it had been natural that he partner with her. Quinn and Leila had paired up. Aisling was too scared to look over at them lest she and Leila have one of their giggle attacks. She wouldn't have been able to keep a straight face were it Quinn currently gyrating in front of her. It was all very well and good getting down and dirty when you had fiery Cuban blood rushing through your veins. It was a little trickier above a shop on Dame Street in Ireland, home to the Irish jig.

'What brings you here?' Marcus asked, attempting to spin her around.

'My friend, the blonde girl over there in green, thought it would be fun,' Aisling whispered shuffling her feet along to the tempo. To her surprise, she was picking up the steps and managing to keep time with the rhythm. She was, she realised, having fun. She risked a glance at Leila and Quinn. Leila was gazing down at her feet as though surprised to discover she had two left ones. Quinn though, she noticed, watching him for a few beats, was a natural. Who'd have thought?

She was glad Marcus was no Fred Astaire and had wound up here at Lozano's Dance Studio. She'd already decided tonight was going to be worth her not being able to move in the morning. It wasn't going to be down to her having used new muscles, as she attempted moves she hadn't known existed. It had been a long time since she'd shaken her booty with as much enthusiasm as she was currently doing. No, her immobility would be because of her poor feet. She'd already lost count of how many times Marcus had trodden on them! Ah well, she thought stealing a glance at him from under her lashes, he had warned her.

'How do you manage it?'

'What?'

'Dancing in those shoes. Staying upright must be a challenge in itself.'

'Practice.' Aisling grinned. She really was enjoying herself and was pleased she'd let her friend talk her into coming. Wednesday night salsa classes were going to be fun.

'Ah, I see. That's the secret then. So what do you do?' Marcus asked.

'I manage my family's guest house on St Stephen's Green, O'Mara's.

'I know it.'

She wasn't surprised. O'Mara's was a fixture on the Dublin landscape.

'Until a couple of months ago I was working in resort management. My last post was near Hania in Crete. It's a stunning part of the world. Have you been?'

He shook his head and frowned. 'No, I usually head for Cyprus. You came back to take over the family business?'

'It was that, or it was going to be sold. My dad died, and Mammy decided she needed a fresh start. It's taking a bit to settle back in, but the guesthouse is home.'

'I'm sorry about your dad.'

She smiled to let him know it was okay. 'What about you, what do you do?'

'I'm a manager at AIB.'

'A salsa dancing bank manager.'

He groaned, 'That was never on my CV, but you know I think I might have to thank Madeline for making me come along tonight.'

They smiled at one another and Aisling felt a shiver of anticipation that tonight was the start of something special.

~

Across the room Quinn was amazed. His feet had taken on a life of their own once the music had started and he was following Antonio's instructions with ease. He glanced over at Aisling. He'd only agreed to come to these classes because it was a chance to be close to her. He could see how this was going to go though. He'd seen it the moment her face had lit up when that eejit, Ricky Martin wannabe, who was wiggling his hips in front of her had walked into the room.

'Quinn get off my foot,' Leila yelped.

# Chapter 14

'Aisling O'Mara, how long until Marcus makes an honest woman of you?'

Aisling blinked, realising she was still holding the coins she'd dug out of her purse for the busker in her hand. She tossed them into the violin case acknowledging his grateful smile before turning her attention to her old classmate, Orla.

'Hi, Orla. Gosh, it's been ages.' She gave her old chum a hug. 'Two weeks to go. I've just been for my final fitting tonight.' She filled Orla in on what was planned for the day itself, feeling a stab of guilt that she hadn't invited her. The cost per head for the meal meant she'd had to be ruthless and bypass friends she didn't see on a regular basis. Mammy had twittered on about inviting Mrs so-and-so, and Mrs you-remember-her Aisling—but she'd stood firm. She'd done the same with Mrs McDonagh. She'd had to because Marcus seemed to have taken a backseat where their big day was concerned. Content to let her do all the organising, and that included dealing with his mam!

Orla's husband, Eddie, appeared alongside them with a familiar green M&S bag in his hand. He said hello to Aisling and stood listening to her and his wife catching up, beginning to shuffle his feet impatiently after a while. Orla took the hint and wished Aisling the best of luck for her big day before the two women said their goodbyes.

Nina was manning the front desk when Aisling breezed through the door, having made a mental note to polish the brass nameplate in the morning.

'How's things, Nina?' she asked the younger Spanish girl who was clipping papers into a ring binder. She'd worked at O'Mara's for the last few months.

'Ola. We're quiet tonight, Aisling. Marcus called in though, he left this.' She produced an envelope which Aisling curiously took from her outstretched hand.

Marcus had known she wasn't going to be in this afternoon. She'd told him she was meeting Moira and Leila for their final fitting. He was supposed to be going for the suit fitting she'd arranged for him. His pants were too long and would definitely need taking up. It surprised her he'd found time to swing by O'Mara's. She itched to get upstairs to see what was inside the envelope not wanting to open it in front of Nina in case it was something that would make her blush. Unlikely, given Marcus's practical nature, but you never knew.

'How did the fitting go? I can't wait to see your dress,' Nina smiled.

'It went well, not much to tweak at all, although it is a little snug around here.' She patted her middle and Nina laughed.

'I'm sure it'll be fine.'

The envelope was like a hot potato in her hand, but she hovered a tick longer to ask Nina how her family was. There was a quiet sadness about the young girl at times and Aisling put it down to her being homesick. Her pretty face always grew animated when she spoke of her family. She knew that work was scarce in the small town where Nina came from especially in the cooler months. Dublin, with its boom, had guaranteed her employment and a chance to perfect her English.

'My madre and padre are talking about extending their restaurante,' she said. Aisling had heard all about the small family-owned restaurant in the old town of Toledo where they lived. She also knew Nina sent money home to her parents. She worked two jobs, the evening shift here at O'Mara's Monday to Friday from four until ten pm. It was Nina who locked up of an evening, getting a taxi, on O'Mara's tab, home to the house she shared with six others. In the day she waitressed a lunchtime shift at popular Pedro's in Temple Bar.

Nina began telling her about how her mother made the best cocido madrileño, and that there was nothing better to warm yourself with when the weather grew cool. Aisling's mouth watered hearing all about the pork stew with its chorizo sausage and chickpeas which simmered for hours. She hadn't had any dinner and the crumbs she'd snaffled from Leila's plate hardly counted. The phone rang, and their conversation drew to a close.

Aisling gave Nina a wave and raced up the stairs to the apartment. She let herself in, flicking on the light as she closed the door behind her. It wasn't quite dark yet, but rather that hazy in-between greyish light that signalled night was drawing in. The street lights had yet to come on she noticed, quickly drawing the curtains before kicking her shoes off and curling up in her chair by the window. Only once she was comfortable did she open the envelope, then she tore into it in anticipation of what it might contain.

Perhaps Marcus had picked up the tickets for their honeymoon. They'd booked ten days of lazing in the sun, snorkelling, delicious food, and languid lovemaking in a luxury villa in the Maldives, bliss.

It wasn't tickets, however, and she unfolded the plain piece of white paper curiously, her eyes skimming Marcus's familiar neat handwriting. She could read the words, but she couldn't comprehend what they meant.

*Ash, this isn't an easy letter for me to write and I know that not telling you to your face is cowardly. I'm ashamed of myself for writing this but if I tried to sit down with you to say I can't go through with the wedding, I'd bottle it. I wouldn't be able to stand the hurt on your face. You see, I knew I'd made a mistake from the moment I slid the diamond on your finger, but I couldn't see a way back.*

*My only excuse is things spiralled out of control these past months. I've felt like I was on a conveyor belt and I couldn't get off. I do love you, please know that, but I shouldn't have proposed to you. It was too soon, and I wasn't ready. I'm not sure I'll ever be ready, to be honest. I've seen what marriage has done to my parents. They've lived a life of bitterness and sniping. I was always stuck in the middle of it and I'm sure they only stayed together for my sake. Then when I grew up, they stayed out of habit. I don't want us to wind up like that.*

*Why did I ask you to marry me then? All I can say is I knew it was what you wanted, and I wanted to make you happy. In doing so I've only succeeded in ultimately making you unhappy. Leaving Dublin seems the kindest thing to do. I'm transferring to Cork. I'm sorry from the bottom of my heart and I hope one day you'll see it was the right thing for me to do.*

*Marcus*

# Chapter 15
# Present Day

Aisling peered at her face in the bathroom mirror. Her eyes were swollen thanks to the tears she'd shed poring over Marcus's letters last night. If she had a dollar for every tear she'd cried since he'd left, she'd be a wealthy woman, she thought as she cursed him under her breath. She'd sat at the table last night unable to stop torturing herself, again reading through every word he'd written to her these last few months until she reached the beginning, or the end, however you wanted to look at it.

All those hard-edged raw emotions at the knowledge he was leaving, and her life was not going to move forward from the sixth of September as Mrs McDonagh, had rained down on her once more like cold wet sleet.

There would be no fairy tale day, with a happily ever after. There'd be no husband at her side, helping her run O'Mara's in the same fashion Mammy and Dad had. The third bedroom in the apartment would remain empty and untouched. It wouldn't be painted in a sunny yellow with a Winnie the Pooh border, in anticipation of needing a nursery. She would continue to live here with Moira; her life would go on as it had before she'd attended that salsa class and met Marcus.

Aisling knew she'd survive, but she felt like a rug had been wrenched out from under her feet. Those first couple of months after Marcus had run away with his tail between his legs had been a period in her life she'd never have navigated her way through if it wasn't for Leila and Quinn. Again, they were the two sane constants who were there for her when life had let her down.

It was all well and good with Mammy, Roisin—who'd caught the first flight out of London upon hearing the news—and Moira railing against Marcus but it didn't achieve anything. Although she'd admit there was a certain satisfaction to be gleaned from hearing them call him everything under the sun while she sat and cried. It didn't change the facts though, she'd still been deserted. While her family had ranted and raved in between consoling her, it was Leila who'd stepped up and taken practical control of the situation.

'This is the story, right?' she'd told the O'Mara women looking fierce for such a delicately boned woman. 'Aisling and Marcus the fecker, you're not to actually say that by the way, mutually concluded they weren't right for each other after all.' They'd all nodded gratefully at Leila glad somebody was telling them what they should say and do.

It was like one of those official celebratory breakup announcements—all very civilised and mutual. Aisling was clinging to the word 'mutual'. Mutual was her mantra because it meant she could continue to show her face around town. Despite her fragile state of mind she still had enough wits about her to tell her friend if she ever got fed up with the wedding business, she'd make a fortune in public relations.

Leila had set about telephoning their guests and if anybody had questioned the eleventh-hour cancellation notice she'd replied smartly with, 'Sure look it, isn't it better this way than realising they weren't right for each other six months down the line?' She'd negotiated the return of deposits through the promise of recommending future business to those left in the last-minute lurch. In short, she'd pulled Aisling out of a very big hole with her dignity intact. So while her heart may have been broken at least she could hold her head up.

'Should I go to Cork, see if I can make some sense out of all of this?' Aisling had asked over the top of her sugary cup of tea the third morning after Marcus had absconded. She'd been living on sugary cups of tea and not much else since she'd read the note. Quinn upon hearing she wasn't eating had been acting as *Meals on Wheels*. He was adamant he could tempt even the most finicky of eaters but all she could think about was Marcus. The urge to confront him—to see him one last time and ask him how he could do this to her, was all consuming.

'No, you should not!' Moira, Roisin, and Mammy chimed. 'Have some pride!'

'If anybody's going to Cork, it's me. I'll sort the fecker.' Fighting words from Moira.

'And me,' added Mammy, not to be beaten. 'I'll show him what I think of him.'

Roisin simply shrugged, 'I'm not going. I'm a lover, not a fighter. I'll stay here and look after you, Ash, while those two go and deal with him.'

'Nobody is going to Cork. Marcus made himself quite clear in the note as to how he felt. What's our catchphrase, Aisling?' Leila looked to Aisling like a conductor his choir.

'If someone you love hurts you, cry a river, build a bridge, and get over it.'

'Ooh, that's good, where did you find it?' Roisin asked.

'Online, under quotes to heal broken hearts, it's anonymous. Aisling's to keep repeating it to herself. The power of positive thinking and all that.'

Now, Aisling wiped away the steam her breath had left on the mirror as she said the words out loud to the face staring back at her. She'd cried the river, she'd spent the last year building a bridge, but having seen Marcus yesterday, she knew she was far from over it. Ah God, a thought occurred to her, would he call this morning? He would be back—she knew he would and the uncertainty of when he would next appear had her nerves jangling.

*Why couldn't he have stayed in Cork?* she asked herself again as she was filled by an urge to run away. Oh, to pack a bag and head for the hills, or even better back to Crete. She closed her eyes for a beat, picturing herself back walking the streets of Hania's shaded old town, pausing to buy olives and a loaf of crusty bread. She couldn't run away because she'd made a commitment to her family by coming back and stepping into Mammy's shoes. She'd been raised to keep her promises, and if she were to break hers now, she'd be no better than Marcus fecking coward McDonagh!

Aisling turned away from the mirror. She needed to get moving, starting with a hot shower. That would surely have a restorative effect. It did and she felt better once she'd towelled off and dressed. Her careful make-up application made her look much more herself and she was hopeful her puffy eyes would have gone down by the time she got on the train to Howth. She'd pop downstairs and see how the land lay shortly. Hopefully, Mr Fox had behaved himself last night and there would be no disgruntled Una Brennan to deal with. First things first, though, she'd wake Moira and remind her they were off to meet Mammy for lunch.

She knocked on her sister's door and waited. In days of old she would have barrelled on in but she'd learned her lesson the hard way having caught her sister in flagrante delicto with her ex-boyfriend. Her face still flamed at the memory—*when had her baby sister grown up? And more importantly what was she doing bringing her boyfriend back here to the family home?*

Moira once dressed and with the boyfriend sent packing, had pointed out loudly that she afforded Aisling the courtesy of knocking before entering and she should do the same. She'd also said what was good for the goose was good for the gander. Which in English meant if Aisling was happy to ride Marcus as though she were trying to win the Irish Derby under the O'Mara family roof then Moira was entitled to do the same.

Aisling had protested that Mammy would go mad if she'd known all this riding was going on and at least Marcus was making an honest woman of her. Moira had tossed this remark aside with a casual, 'Well what Mammy doesn't know won't hurt her.'

The ground rules for living together as adult siblings with no parents to lay down the law was murky territory indeed, Aisling concluded, backing down.

Today thankfully there was no sound of anything untoward coming from her sister's room other than her familiar snores. The loudness of which meant she'd given it a good nudge last night. Aisling shook her head. She'd always kept a wary eye out for Moira, and it was a hard habit to break. She knew too that Moira would have loved to have been out from under her overprotective feet, free to do what she wanted without her sister eyeballing her disapprovingly, but the soaring rents in the city since the Celtic Tiger had begun to roar and the economy boomed made sure it wasn't an option.

Aisling was secretly glad, even if Moira and her diva attitude did drive her mad sometimes. She wouldn't have liked to have been left to rattle around in the manor house's apartment on her lonesome.

She knocked louder and waited a few seconds longer before opening the door.

'Jaysus, it smells like a pub in here.' She waved her hand under her nose before opening the curtains, so she could let some air into the room.

Moira stirred, squinting at the light before pulling the sheet over her head. 'Shut the curtains.'

'I will not, we're meeting Mammy for lunch remember?'

'But I'm in bits, Ash. I can't possibly go. I think I've picked up a tummy bug.'

'You'll feel better after a shower.'

Moira disentangled herself from the sheet and sat up.

She would not win the Rose of Tralee at this moment in time, thought Aisling.

Moira groaned. 'I feel sick like a small hospital.'

'The best cure for the brown bottle flu is a hot shower, some paracetamol, and one of Mrs Flaherty's full Irish's.' Aisling was annoyed, she'd told Moira not to overdo it and so she served her ace. 'Hmm I'll ask her to whip you up a nice runny egg with lashings of black pudding, shall I?'

Moira turned green, but it had the desired effect and she leaped from her bed.

# Chapter 16

U na sipped her tea, and her eyes flicked to the younger O'Mara sister who was sitting across the dining room from her. Mrs Flaherty was fussing around her, clearly fond of the girl. She was pretty that was for sure, with her flashing dark eyes and shiny hair. A real head-turner, but then so was Aisling, the manageress. They certainly weren't peas in a pod though. If Una were a betting woman, she'd say there'd been lots of jokes about the milkman having come-a-calling over the years. Although, stealing another glance over, if you looked closely you could tell the two were sisters. It was in the shape of their faces and the tilt of their noses.

It was also apparent from the younger sister's greenish tinge, she was under the weather. Out on the sauce last night no doubt, serves her right. Una, who never touched a drop, was prim. The younger generation were far too fond of getting on the, *what did they call it?* she searched for the word she'd overheard the two young lads use on the train—*lash,* that was it.

Una liked to listen in on young people's conversation. She'd tune in as she stood in the queue at the Tesco's or when she was waiting at the station. The bus and the train were good places in which to catch snippets of banter. She was out of touch with their generation in a way, when she was young, she'd never have dreamed possible. Language was a funny thing the way words came and went like hem lengths over the years. So was age, she thought, eyeing the liver spots on the back of her hand.

She wondered if this young lass, who under Mrs Flaherty's watchful eye was dipping her toast into her egg yolk, knew what it was to have her heart broken. Or, was she the one who did the heart breaking?

Una had been a pretty girl once too. Leo used to tell her she was beautiful. He used to tell her she made his heart sing. He was a man of hearts and flowers was Leo. Why then if he'd thought her beautiful and she made his heart sing hadn't she been enough?

She sighed and put her teacup down in the saucer. It was all such a long time ago but if she shut her eyes, the pain was as fresh as the day it had been inflicted. Her mind was prone to drift and she'd find herself back in that moment. Why was it so hard to remember if she'd put the cat out before she went to bed of a night, but the events of April 12, 1950, were as vivid as a film being projected onto the big screen?

She could hear the rustle of fabric as Mrs Flaherty made her way over, pulling her from her thoughts as she nodded her greeting. The cook's smile was tight as she asked if everything was to her liking. Una felt a pang. She didn't want to be this awkward old woman whom people tiptoed around. It was a role however she'd begun to play with such tenacity she'd forgotten how to let her guard down.

'It's fine, thank you,' she replied, pleased she'd had the foresight to order the Continental today. She'd managed the small bowl of cereal she'd helped herself to from the buffet as well as a slice of wholemeal toast. She could have complimented the woman on the marmalade which she was certain was homemade, but she remained tight-lipped. Mrs Flaherty looked as if she'd liked to say something but thought better of it, taking herself off to the kitchen instead.

Today Una vowed she'd knock on Aideen's door. She wouldn't while away the hours sitting in the park across the road from her sister's house. Sitting on the bench like some sort of stalker as she watched the comings and goings—trying to catch a glimpse of her nephews. They'd be approaching middle-age now with children who were no doubt at that age where they had their parents tearing their hair out. What a thought! Her a great-aunt.

The problem was, once she got to the street on which Aideen had spent the last thirty or so years of her life, she couldn't bring herself to knock on her door. She'd told herself that she'd brazen it out yesterday, and the day before. Time was running out, but each day sitting on that hard bench she'd felt like she'd gazed at Medusa's face and been turned to stone.

# Chapter 17

A isling stared out the window to the pocket-sized gardens rushing by below. Their smalls, and not so small's, blowing on the breeze for all to see. Her view beyond these yards was blocked by row after row of pebble-dashed houses all whizzing past in uniform design. She was facing backwards and feeling queasy on it. She hated not sitting facing the direction in which she was travelling on any kind of public transport, but the train had been packed when they'd boarded it. The only two seats left were situated diagonally from each other. She and Moira had stared at the empty spaces for a beat before having a stand-off over who was sitting where. They were obliviously providing entertainment to the bored passengers as they bickered back and forth.

'For the love of Jaysus, sit down the pair of you.' A man with a missing front tooth wheezed.

Moira looked as though she were going to tell him to mind his own business as she glanced at him sharply. She closed her mouth though, deciding to save her depleted energy reserves for her mammy and not waste them on a verbal exchange with a stranger. Aisling finally conceded to sit where she was currently perched because her sister was clearly still green around the gills. She didn't want to have to help clean it up if she lost the contents of her stomach, a very real possibility. Mind you she wasn't feeling too flash herself.

She'd clambered over the elderly woman with her handbag on her knee, resolutely refusing to move across and make her life easier. 'I like an aisle seat,' she said, once Aisling collapsed huffing and puffing into her seat. *Bully for you*, she said to herself trying not to think about the slice of chocolate fudge cake she'd wolfed down not half an hour ago. Mr Walsh had left the promised piece of cake at reception for her and she'd shovelled it down when James took himself off to the gents because she didn't want to share.

As the train lurched forward, she glanced over to where Moira was sitting. Her legs were twisted toward the aisle, and she had a look of concentration on her face as she breathed in and out slowly. She met her sister's gaze and Aisling shot her a look that said she'd kill her if she showed them up by hurling on public transport.

Despite the odds being stacked against them, they made the journey without incident. Aisling exhaled, relieved as the train slowed and came to a halt in Howth Station. The sisters joined the throng exiting the train, hearing the excited chattering of plans being made for the day. They were keen, Aisling guessed, to make the most of the glorious weather and spend the day with the whiff of salt air in their nostrils.

The crowd carried them along until they exited down the steps of the pretty station building, its hanging baskets either side of the wooden doors a profusion of tumbling pinks and reds. Aisling looked down the street; she could hear the snapping of the flags flying outside The Bloody Stream, its front beer garden and spiky cabbage palm trees lending a festive and determined air to hang onto the last vestiges of summer.

She averted her eyes away from the pub. Marcus had brought her there once not long after he'd proposed. She'd admired the diamond in her ring as it caught the light waving her hand about in conversation far more than was necessary. The interior, she recalled, was rustic and cosy and the craic had been great. There'd been live music; she'd wanted to dance but Marcus wasn't keen. She'd also tasted the best bowl of chowder she'd eaten in her life. If Mammy suggested they go there for lunch though, she'd have to refuse on the basis of painful memories. It was a shame because the chowder had been delicious. She realised she was feeling better now as her mouth watered at the thought of the creamy soup. She scanned the faces of people walking toward the station and her eyes soon fixed on Mammy who was waving out like a mad thing.

'Ahoy there, me hearties,' Moira muttered.

'Shush, she looks very well on it.' Aisling couldn't help but grin though; she did look like a feminine version of Captain Birdseye, without the beard of course! Still, it was nice to see her with her rounded figure of old. She'd gotten awfully thin after Dad died. She was looking much more her old self these days, even if this new version did insist on wearing casual sailing get-up for every occasion. It was a blessing she didn't wear a white cap and smoke a pipe to complete her look.

'Hi, Mammy! I like your hair.' Aisling eyed her mammy's shoulder-length bob, the hair lightened to a mid-brown with reddish-undertones. It was softer than her natural dark, almost black, colour which she guessed would be peppered with grey these days. Aisling hugged her as she caught up to them.

Mammy appeared to have shrunk in the few weeks since Aisling had last seen her. It took a beat for her to realise it was the flat shoes. She'd taken to wearing them since moving to the seaside village. Maureen released her daughter before giving her the once over. 'You're looking good, Aisling. I like the shoes although probably not the most practical pick for a stroll along the pier. And you could do with getting those ends trimmed yourself.' She picked up a handful of her daughter's reddish gold hair and frowned. 'Yes, a little trim, I think. Treena, my stylist is marvellous. A little pricey but well worth it.' She swished her hair around for Aisling and Moira to admire.

Aisling had to smile at her mammy's use of the word stylist. She obviously thought it sounded posh because she'd rolled the sentence off her tongue with a plummy tone. 'Alright, Mammy, I'll book myself in for a cut.' Thirty-four years old and she was still doing as she was told!

Mollified, Maureen O'Mara turned her attention to her youngest child pulling her down into a busty embrace.

'Mam, let me go. I can't breathe,' Moira's muffled voice wafted up from the depths of her cleavage. 'Jaysus,' she muttered once released, 'you just about knocked me out. I can see the headline, 'Dublin girl rendered unconscious in a seaside village by mammy's overuse of Arpège. You'll have Ireland's bee population trying to pollinate you smelling like that.'

Maureen ignored Moira's diatribe as her eyes raked over her, narrowing as they settled on her face. 'You've a look of Princess Fiona about you—the ogress version. On the lash last night, were we?' She didn't wait for a reply. 'Just the other day I was reading an article in the paper about the young people of our country's disturbing drinking habits. To think my own daughter plays a part in those drunken statistics.' She shook her head. Aisling wasn't sure if it was done in dismay over her daughter's drinking habits or whether she just wanted to swish her hair around again.

'You're a fine one to talk, Mammy. I can remember you singing Danny Boy at the top of your lungs when you'd knocked back a few sherries with Kate Finnegan.'

'Don't be cheeky, t'was only the once. Come on now we've a reservation at Aqua, it's only been opened a year. I've not been before but I've heard good things about it from my golfing ladies.'

The sisters linked arms with their mammy and to Aisling's relief bypassed The Bloody Stream as they turned toward Dublin Bay instead. The water was calm and blue despite the wind that whipped around them as they stepped out onto the pier. Aisling filled her lungs with the tangy air. The fresh sea breeze would sort Moira out too. She watched the fishing boats jiggling against one another on their pier-side moorings. On the other side of the walkway, smart sailing boats were showcased in the marina. Determined anglers were fishing off the side of the pier and families were strolling its length. The lighthouse loomed at the end of the jetty guarding the entrance to Howth Harbour. It was a symbolic welcome and farewell to weary travellers, Aisling always thought somewhat romantically.

Aqua was housed inside the former Howth Sailing Club building. 'You should feel right at home in here Mammy, what with you looking the part and all,' Moira said holding the door open for her.

Maureen wasn't sure whether Moira was being sarcastic or not so she shot her a fierce look to be on the safe side. They were ushered to a table near the expansive windows and she announced loudly for the benefit of the other diners that they had a prime table. 'Just look at that sea view would you girls.'

As Moira and Aisling skimmed over the menu, she filled them in on her latest news. Derbhilla her golfing partner was having her knees done on Thursday. She was going to be out of action for a month or so. Maureen had been making up meals to pop in her friend's freezer for her to have when she got home from the hospital. 'Her husband's as useless as a chocolate teapot,' she confided moving swiftly onto her frenemy, Agnes. She was a fellow widow who was making noises about stepping into Derbhilla's shoes while she was out of action. 'She's got far too much to say for herself in my opinion and I'm on the fence about her scoring abilities. I've a sneaking suspicion she doctors her results to better her handicap.'

Things could get ugly on the Deer Park Ladies golf course, Aisling smiled to herself, deciding on pan fried fillet of fish. She'd be strong and bypass a starter but she thought, perusing the desserts, she'd share the sticky toffee pudding with Mammy for afters. It was their favourite.

By the time the waiter came to take their order they'd also received a blow-by-blow account of Rosemary Farrell's—a member of Mammy's rambling group—recent hip operation. *Who knew the metal orthopaedic implant could set the airport detectors off?* Apparently, Rosemary had learned this the hard way—holding all and sundry up at Dublin Airport as she tried to pass through security. She'd been patted down three times by the overly enthusiastic security guard, although Maureen said it was probably the most excitement Rosemary had had in years!

Moira not surprisingly ordered the fish and chips with pea purée. A good dose of stodge to soak up her sins.

'Sure, the purée will match your face,' Mammy muttered, before announcing that she'd like the steak. 'And shall we get a bottle of wine girls?'

Moira groaned.

'That'd be nice, Mammy,' Aisling said. It wasn't as though she'd be driving anywhere, and she hadn't overdone it last night, far from it. She'd taken herself off to bed, all cried out, with a mug of sweet tea hoping it would send her off to the land of nod. Not that she'd needed any help sleeping, she'd been exhausted. As the waiter scurried off with their orders and the promise of a chilled bottle of house white upon his return. Aisling decided now would be as good a time as any to tell her mammy and sister that Marcus was back in town.

# Chapter 18

Moira choked on the water she'd just taken a sip of as Mammy thrust a napkin at her. 'You've dribble on your chin, Moira, wipe it up.'

'Did you just say Marcus is back in town?' She turned her attention to Aisling.

Aisling nodded, the shock had worn off in the ensuing hours that had passed since she'd seen him. But she could see how it had taken them by surprise. She filled them in on how she'd spotted him making a beeline for O'Mara's and how she'd successfully avoided him.

'Good woman,' Mammy said when Aisling told her how Bronagh had embellished her social life by telling him she wouldn't be home later either. Thus getting her off the hook yesterday at least.

'I need this,' Aisling said as the waiter returned and set about pouring the wine.

Moira, having decided the news that had just been imparted warranted a hair of the dog, held her glass up to be filled too.

'He's a chancer, that one.' Mammy shook her head doing the hair swishy thing once more.

'It's a good thing I wasn't there when he called,' Moira rasped. 'I'd have eaten the head off him, so I would.'

'I'm going to have to see him.' Aisling owned up to the letters he'd been sending her. 'If I'd replied he might have stayed away.'

'I don't think it would have made any difference, Ash. He's a spoiled only child, who's far too used to getting his own way. Just tell him to feck right off next time he shows up.'

Aisling couldn't help but think Moira's take on Marcus was a touch ironic given her own uncanny ability of getting what she wanted when she wanted it. Still, that was their own faults for running around after her the way they had when she was a tot. Marcus perhaps *was* used to things going his way, but that didn't make him a bad person.

'Aisling, what is running through that head of yours?' Mammy's eyes narrowed. 'You get the same expression on your face whenever Mrs Flaherty makes noises about seeing that auld fox off. You're a soft touch. Always have been.'

Aisling took a big gulp of her wine. She needed fortification if she was going to be honest about what was on her mind. 'Mammy, I need to see him. I don't expect either of you to understand but it might give me the closure I need.'

Moira muttered under her breath and Aisling was sure she caught the words feck and sake in there.

Mammy was more vocal. 'You're not guest starring on Oprah,' she shouted. 'We don't use words like journey and closure in our family. They are banned, bad words, do you hear me? We say things like on your bike you weasel and, and—'

'Feck off, fecker with the little pecker.' Moira waggled her little finger for effect.

Aisling shot Moira a look. 'Not helpful and not true, as it happens.'

'Well, what do you expect?' Moira said.

'But what if he is genuinely sorry? I mean he wouldn't be the first man to get cold feet before his wedding now, would he? What if he wants to put things right between us? He might want to apologise to my face, Mammy. I'd like to hear him say he was sorry.' Her words sounded cringeworthy even to her own ears.

Several diners' heads spun in their direction at Moira and Mammy's eruption but Moira wasn't finished. 'That gob shite flicked you off with a note, Aisling. A note! He didn't even have the decency to call the wedding off to your face. We were there to pick up the pieces not him. He does not deserve a second chance of any kind!'

Aisling's face flamed. 'Would you two lower the volume, the whole of Aqua does not need to know I was dumped, thank you very much.'

Their waiter, arriving with her pan-fried fish balanced in one hand and Moira's fish and chips in the other, was a welcome distraction. Aisling wasn't sure if she was imagining it or not, but he seemed to be extra solicitous toward her. He fluffed about shaking out her napkin and draping it on her lap before asking if she'd like an extra serving of tartare sauce on the house, or a top up of her wine, perhaps?

She knew she wasn't imagining it when he patted her shoulder and said, 'The same thing happened to my sister one week before she was due to walk down the aisle. She's moved on now, married a fella from up the road in Malahide. He's a face on him like a bag of spuds but plenty of dosh.' He pointed out the window, 'That's his yacht there the big shiny one. So you see, life does go on. You'll be alright, love.'

Oh for God's sake! Aisling was puce. So the moral of his story was she could look forward to marrying someone ugly with pots of money and a yacht—bloody great!

Mammy jumped in, 'And tell me now—' she cast around for his name.

'Boyd,' he offered up.

'Boyd. What would your sister have done if that eejit ex of hers had made noises about patching things up?'

He looked around to make sure no guests were within earshot and leaned in toward the party of three. 'She'd have told him he was a ballbag and sent him packing. With said bollocks between his knees.'

'There you go, Aisling. That's what you're to do.' Mammy and Moira were united in victory.

Then like the sun coming out from behind the clouds, Mammy's face cleared. She turned toward Boyd, giving him the benefit of her smile set at full wattage as she asked him, would there be any chance of an introduction to his sister and her husband. 'Only I'm after sailing lessons and was looking to meet some like-minded boaties.'

~

It was later sitting on the DART home, bellies full and with that warm glow of having partaken of a tipple at lunchtime, that Aisling thought to ask her sister how her night had been. They were both in better spirits on the return journey thanks to Aisling facing forward and Moira's hangover having disappeared over the course of lunch. She'd texted her friend Andrea to see if she still wanted to catch up, after checking with Aisling whether she wanted her to come home with her in case Marcus was there.

Aisling knew Moira was desperate to look for a dress to wear to the snooty engagement party she'd been invited to. Besides, Moira bopping Marcus on the nose if she came face-to-face with him wouldn't do any good. She had to be the grown up he'd failed to be and talk to him face-to-face. It was inevitable he'd show up at some point and she refused to skulk around like she had yesterday while she waited for him to reappear.

She told Moira this and knowing the shops would still be open by the time their train rolled back into the city, her sister arranged to jump off at Connolly Station. Andrea would meet her there and they could hunt for their outfits before going for an early dinner and then seeing where the evening led them. It was Saturday night, after all—she looked meaningfully at Aisling when she said this.

Aisling ignored the look. How Moira could think about food after the lunch they'd just put away was beyond her. Come to think of it, how she could think about hitting the town again after the state she'd been in this morning was incomprehensible. Oh to be young and have stamina she thought before moving on. Her curiosity piqued as to whether Moira had had any success in batting her eyelashes in Liam Shaughnessy, the Asset Management bigwig's, direction.

'What did you get up to last night then?' she asked. 'Did you try your luck with yer man?'

'Liam?' She pulled a face. 'No, he fancies the pants off himself, so he does and besides, he copped off with Mary from litigation. There's no accounting for taste.'

'That's an about turn. Yesterday you were all googly eyed over him.'

Moira's look was withering. 'Ah well, now that's because I've seen the light. Good luck to Mary, I say. She's batting above her weight there, but I've got my eye on a more mature man. A silver fox no less.'

'Jaysus, Moira you're not after getting yourself a sugar daddy, are you?' Aisling mentally flicked through the images of the managing partners she'd seen on the company's website. The only lawyer who stood out amongst the montage was the fella she'd thought looked like he should be wearing a tall green hat. 'Please tell me it's not yer man I said looked like a leprechaun?'

'No, and Mr Sweeney looks like Mr Wonka, not a leprechaun, you're confused. We had that discussion.'

'Well, who then?' She'd expected an angry, or at the very least quick off the mark, rebuttal as to her suggestion of a sugar daddy. Moira, however, smiled enigmatically, reminding Aisling of the Mona Lisa.

She knew she wouldn't glean anything further from her; her sister was enjoying being mysterious too much. So she turned her attention to the rows of pocket-sized gardens once more. She hoped the owners of the sheets billowing on the breeze, brought them in before that dark cloud she could see lurking ominously on the horizon blew over top of their gardens. A shiver passed through her and she hoped that cloud wasn't an omen.

# Chapter 19

U na Brennan sat on the bench with her cardigan wrapped tightly around her. The sun might be out, but the breeze had a bite. There was a cloud in the distance too, it was dark and heavy. She didn't like the look of it and hoped it didn't decide to blow over in her direction. Despite the unusual clemency of the day she was cold, chilled to the bone from sitting in the same spot as she had done each day since arriving in Dublin.

The park was gated and the bench where she was seated was overhung by a tree from which the odd orange leaf floated down to land at her feet. Small children were shrieking as they clambered up the slide or bounced on the see-saw. Beyond the gates and across the road was a row of red brick houses, not dissimilar to the one in which she'd grown up. In the middle of that row was the house that belonged to Aideen.

*What was it like inside?* she wondered, recalling how Aideen always kept her side of their bedroom neat as a pin, whereas she'd driven her sister potty with her habit of leaving things wherever they happened to fall. She leaned forward, watching as a car pulled up outside the house, performing a parallel park. It was skilfully done. She'd never mastered the art herself, and many a time had driven straight on ending up miles from where she wanted to be.

A tall chap with a shock of sandy, reddish hair and a middle that was just starting to soften got out of the car. Una gasped.

He looked exactly like their da when he was in his middling years. He had to be one of Aideen's lads there was no doubt. He opened the back door, bending down to re-emerge with a small child in his arm. The wee kiddie had overalls on and his tousled hair, the same colour as his father's, gave away the fact he'd fallen asleep in the back of the car.

Una felt a physical pang, a yearning to call out to them. She wanted them to know her. They'd recognise her certainly but what would she say? She wished she could push rewind, go back and do things differently this time around.

Behind her a swing creaked and she remembered how she'd loved the swings as a girl. *Higher, higher!* she'd order Aideen who'd obligingly push her. She'd kick her legs out imagining she could see over the stacks of chimney pots to the seaside beyond. If she swung hard enough her magic swing would take her to the pebbly shore and she'd dip her toes in the icy water, playing catch me if you can with the waves. Una closed her eyes, remembering.

# Chapter 20
# 1942

'That boy in Mrs Greene's front garden is staring at us again, Una,' Aideen whispered. Her lowered voice full of excitement at this unusual turn of events. 'I wonder why he's not in school.' She paused once they were out of his earshot to bend down and pull her ankle sock up. It kept rolling down and disappearing inside her Mary Jane in the most annoying manner. 'I wish my shoe would stop trying to eat my sock,' she said straightening and jiggling her satchel, so the strap would stop digging into her shoulder. It was heavy with the weight of the books she carried.

The Brennan twins were on their way home from school. Mrs Greene lived six doors down from their house in the row of red brick terrace houses where the sisters had lived their entire lives to date. All the houses had bay windows and front doors with shiny brass knockers. It was a matter of pride, Una knew, to make sure your door knocker gleamed. She'd been sent out to polish theirs often enough! To say the boy was standing in the front garden was a stretch of the imagination too. He was leaning on the railings in front of the square patch of grass to the left of the path leading to Mrs Greene's blue door. It had been green until a month ago.

Una risked a glance back over her shoulder. He was still watching them, and she quickly looked away. 'I meant to tell you, but you fell asleep before I could and then I forgot. I heard Mammy telling Daddy last night, he's Mrs Greene's nephew. His mammy's not well so he's come to stay with her. He looks lonely if you ask me. I'd hate to be sent away if our mam was sick. Imagine if we had to go and stay with Aunt Finola?' The thought of their thin-faced spinster aunt who was a firm believer if you spared the rod you spoiled the child, made both girls grimace.

A thought occurred to Una. 'Perhaps they don't have twins where he comes from. Maybe that's why he's staring at us. We're a novelty.' She felt very grown up using a big word like novelty. She'd seen it in a book and had asked Daddy to explain what it meant, storing it away to use at the appropriate time—like now.

'Where do you think he's from?' Aideen's ringlets bounced as she walked the short distance to their front door. She was the quieter and more reserved of the sisters.

'I don't know but I think we ought to find out. If Mammy says we can, let's see if he wants to come to the canal with us to look for eels.'

The smell of stewed tea and the cabbage remnants of last night's colcannon assailed their nostrils as they stepped inside their door. The tea, Una deduced, her nose twitching, meant Mammy's friend Maire had called. She liked her tea brewed strong enough for a mouse to trot on! Tea, Una had overheard her mammy saying had been rationed; Maire would not like that. Una liked to keep an ear out. Adults didn't tell their children very much about anything and listening in was the only way she learned what was going on.

She was sorry she'd missed Maire or Mrs Reynolds as she and Aideen called her, she was a source of wonderment to the sisters. It was in the way she'd weave a story. Even the dullest titbit sounded interesting when relayed by Mrs Reynolds. Whenever she paid a visit, the twins tried to make themselves invisible in the corner of the room so as to be privy to whatever tale she was telling.

The last time she'd called, it had been to show their mam her new coat. She'd leaned in toward Alice and whispered, 'I paid,' she'd looked over her shoulder. Who she thought might be eavesdropping was a puzzle to the girls who were suddenly desperate to know how much she'd paid for her coat. Annoyingly her hand had gone up shielding her mouth as she whispered the figure to Mammy who made an appropriate, oohing sort of noise. It was terribly frustrating but fascinating all at the same time.

Mam had spotted her daughters breaking their necks to try to hear what was being said. 'Maire, we've got ears flapping. Girls go and play.' Yes, most frustrating. The smell of tea had been strong that afternoon too, Una recalled.

Sister Mary Clare had been explaining all about the emergency at school. She said it gave the government special power. She also said that Ireland might be neutral in the war, but they were still feeling the effects with food and fuel shortages. Finbar O'Shea had told them at break he'd heard his parents talking about deer going missing from Phoenix Park. Una wasn't sure if she believed him. So far, her tummy hadn't felt the effects of rationing and right now all she cared about was eels and her soda bread and jam.

Mammy was peeling potatoes at the sink, she had an apron tied around the waist of her floral frock—it seemed to Una she had a frock for each day of the week.

Alice Brennan put her peeler down, wiping her wet hands on her apron as she turned to greet her girls. They'd both swooped on the soda bread she'd put out for them, with its thick smearing of butter and jam, and between bites were full of noisy news about their day at St Mary's. She smiled as Una chattered on over the top of her sister, her eyes wide with the drama of Deirdre O'Malley's misdemeanours. Deirdre, Una said was always scratching her head, and her finger nails were dirty—she hailed from a part of Phibsborough where they didn't care if their doorknockers were shiny. Today she informed her mammy in the self-righteous manner of someone who would never feel the thwack of Sister Mary Clare's wrath, she'd used the ruler when Deirdre answered back.

Una had barely finished relaying her tale before she'd moved on in her typical style.

'Mam, can we go down to the canal to look for eels? We thought we'd ask Mrs Greene's nephew if he wants to come with us. He looks lonely doesn't he, Aideen?'

Aideen nodded, she'd given up on trying to get a word in edgeways and so she contented herself with nibbling on her bread.

'What about your homework?'

'We'll do it as soon as we've helped clear away the dinner things later won't we, Aideen? Sure we only have a little maths to do, anyway.' This wasn't true, they had rather a lot of maths to do but it could wait. She had some very complicated sums to work out in the guise of a shopping list but first things first. Eels!

Alice looked out the window. It was lovely out. It had been so for the last few days; summer it would seem had come early.

The fresh air might burn off Una's boundless energy she decided, agreeing they could head out so long as they were back in plenty of time for dinner. 'Your daddy better not have to come looking for you.' She tried to sound menacing, but their lovely sandy-haired giant of a father was not in the least bit frightening.

'And Una,' Alice added frowning, 'go and put your old cardigan on if you're going to be playing about by the canal. I didn't see you wearing that this morning when you left the house, or I'd have made you go and change.' Her elder daughter could be sneaky at times. She must have smuggled it out in her satchel when she left for school.

'Sorry, Mammy, I only wanted to show Clodagh how pretty it was and how clever you are.' She gave her mammy a winning smile.

When Mammy wasn't cooking or doing some household chore, she had her nose buried in the latest edition of Woman's Own. It was her treat she maintained. It kept her abreast of the goings on in the Royal family and also provided her with the patterns from which she knitted the girls woollens.

'You know better.' Alice didn't come down in the last shower, but she had no wish to take things further this afternoon. She was in too good of a mood, the weather had seen to that. Una, tinker that she was, was walking a thin line after her antics with little Aoife next door though and would be brought into line if she crossed it again.

It was not even a week since Mrs Kelly had rapped on their door as Alice scraped the dinner plates. The woman, who always looked harried, and rightly so given her brood of seven, had her baby dangling off her hip and a tearful Aoife at her side.

'Your Una left Aoife trussed like a chicken to the lamppost and went in for her dinner,' she'd said and Alice could see where Aoife got her tattletale tendencies from.

'Una!' She'd called over her shoulder. She'd heard Bridie Kelly bellowing at her lot next door often enough. An apology was called for from her daughter if she didn't want to feel the lash of her sharp tongue too.

Una had appeared looking sheepish. 'We were only playing cowboys and Indians, Mam.' She demonstrated her war cry before continuing, 'Aoife was my prisoner. I was going to untie her after dinner, only I forgot. Sorry, Aoife.'

Alice bit her lip to stop herself from smiling, Una didn't fool her. She knew young Aoife had told on her one time too many and her daughter knew how to bear a grudge. 'Well, I think you need to tell Aoife you're sorry and sound like you mean it this time, don't you?'

Una had grudgingly acquiesced and peace had been restored but not before she'd gotten a cursory telling off from Alice. She was a wild one at times was Una.

Alice picked up a potato and her peeling knife once more. Una had been told she'd miss out on the family's annual trip to Dublin Zoo if she put one more foot wrong between now and then. That girl of hers thought all she had to do was flash her smile and she'd get off scot free. She shook her head and went back to peeling the spuds.

Una thundered up the stairs; she had no intention of changing. She loved the cardigan's pretty blue colour and its flower border. The soft wool Mammy had knitted it with didn't itch and scratch like her clumpy old yellow one. Oh, she knew alright she wasn't supposed to wear it to school or for playing in, but she also knew it looked well on her and she wanted to impress Mrs Greene's nephew. She looked down at those pretty flowers and felt torn, but only for a second and leaving the hated yellow one in the drawer, she raced back down the stairs.

'Una! How many times have I told you not to run down the stairs? When you break your legs don't coming running to me,' Alice's voice floated out from the kitchen.

Aideen was waiting by their front gate, still chomping on her soda bread. Her eyes widened as her sister flew out the front door. 'Why are you still wearing it? You heard Mammy.'

'My old one's itchy.' She shrugged off Aideen's concern. 'C'mon, he's still there.' She set off down the street, keen to make her getaway and find out more about this newcomer.

Aideen did what she always did and followed behind her sister.

'I'm Una Brennan and this is my sister Aideen. We're twins in case you didn't know. We're both ten,' Una stated boldly, coming to a halt outside Mrs Greene's front gate. Her nephew had moved to sit on the front step and was swinging a chestnut tied to a piece of string back and forth. 'And you can't play conkers on your own.'

'I know that, and it's not called a conker. It's a chessie and I'm the champion at home.'

'Have you not seen twins before?' Aideen piped up, keen to get off on the right foot with this boy.

'Of course, I have, I'm not a culchie.'

Una wasn't sure if she believed him. 'Where are you from then?'

'Cork City. My mam's not well and Da can't look after me as well as her so I've come to stay with my aunt until she's better.'

'Are you an only child then?' This was incomprehensible to Una.

He nodded.

'Well, what's your name?'

'Leo.'

'We're going to look for eels in the canal. Do you want to come, Leo?'

His eyes lit up and shoving his chestnut back in the pocket of his shorts, he stood up.

'You'd better tell Mrs Greene you'll be back in time for your dinner,' Una bossed.

Leo disappeared in the house, reappearing a beat later followed by his aunt.

'Hello, girls.' Mrs Greene's matronly form appeared in the doorway.

'Hello, Mrs Greene.'

'So, you've met young Leo here,' she said looking pleased he'd made some friends. 'He's staying with me awhile and will be starting at Saint Theresa's on Monday.

'You can walk with us to school, Leo, and watch out for Sister Mary Clare she's very fond of her ruler, so she is.'

Ida Greene's mouth twitched, 'Oh I'm sure Leo won't be on the receiving end of that now will you, Leo? He's a good lad.'

Una wasn't so sure, he had a twinkle in his eye that said otherwise.

'Well, you'd best get on your way if you're going to be back for your dinner, and don't fall in the canal any of you! That cardigan's far too pretty to be getting a soaking in there, Una.'

The trio made their way down the street. As they rounded the bend, a huddle of pigeons fighting over slops flapped indignantly back to the rooftop from which they presided over the neighbourhood. Aideen didn't like the pigeons she thought that they might try to peck her. Una informed Leo of this adding that it wasn't the pecking you needed to worry about it was the other sort of deposit that was more of a problem. He laughed, and she felt very pleased with herself.

They kept their eyes open for sticks on the way which could be used to poke at the water, settling for sturdy twigs at the foot of a willow tree. The twins lead the way across the expanse of grass—it was long and tickled their shins—that would take them to the towpath.

'Oh, look at the swans.' Aideen pointed to two regal birds gliding down the water towards the reeds on the other side.

'Here looks a good spot,' Una declared more interested in eels than swans. She made her way to the water's edge and kneeling down began poking at the water with her stick. The other two followed suit.

'I saw a fish!' Leo exclaimed, and the girls gathered around him as he pointed into the green water. Bubbles rose to the surface and Una fancied she caught sight of a tail, but she couldn't be sure.

'What's it like in Cork City then?' she asked, keeping her eyes trained on the water.

Leo told them that from what he could see it wasn't altogether that different from Dublin.

'What's wrong with your mammy?'

'She's something wrong with her heart.'

Aideen squealed. 'There!' A sinewy black shape was just visible before it slithered down into the murky depths.

'Don't lean too close, Una.'

Mindful of falling in, Una poked her stick back in the water to see if she could get it to move again but nothing happened. Time was getting on, they'd best head home if they didn't want to get into trouble. She didn't want to be marched home by Daddy because Mammy would be sure to see her and know she hadn't done as she was told.

Una didn't know how it happened but one minute she was clambering to her feet, brushing the dirt from her knees, the next she had the sleeve of her cardigan snagged on Leo's stick. He jerked it and the wool pulled away with it.

'Stop!' Una shrieked as Aideen got in the mix and tried to disentangle the stick. It was too late though the damage was done. 'Look what you've done. It's my best cardigan,' Una wailed staring at the hole. She burst into tears, there'd be no hiding it from Mammy.

'Sorry, I didn't mean to.' Leo was stricken. 'It was an accident.'

'You should have been more careful!'

Leo walked off, not wanting the twins to see him upset.

'It's not Leo's fault, Una, you shouldn't have shouted at him. You should have worn your old one like Mam told you to.'

Una knew her sister was right, but it didn't help matters. She'd have to sit home on Saturday while the rest of them went to the zoo. She wouldn't get to see her favourite animals, the elephants, and she would not get an ice cream from the hokey-pokey man. She felt sick. Why, oh why hadn't she done as she was told?

It was a subdued duo who made their way back down the streets from which they'd come. They could see Leo in the distance half running, half walking. Una knew she would have to say sorry for the way she'd behaved toward him. She hadn't meant to be horrible, she was angry at herself not him. The fun had gone from the afternoon just like the sun was slipping behind the clouds. Una dragged her heels feeling sicker with each step that took her closer to home.

'I'll tell Mammy it's my one, sure they're identical, aren't they?'

Una felt a flare of hope flicker and then splutter out. 'She won't believe you Aideen, she'll know it was me not listening and doing as I was told.'

'I'll tell her I was showing off,' she nodded toward Leo and Una knew that was exactly what she'd been doing. She'd been showing off by wearing the cardigan. Her sister had her pegged. Aideen knew her as well as she knew herself. 'Come on,' she said. 'Give it to me, and I'll put it on.'

'Thank you.' Una's voice was muffled as she shrugged out of the cardi, knowing she'd never admire the pretty flower border without feeling sick again.

'I wouldn't want to go to the zoo without you anyway,' Aideen said taking it from her and handing Una her old yellow one that itched.

~

# Present Day

U na's thoughts returned to the present, roused by a child's ear-piercing shriek. She glanced over to see the culprit's arms flung out sliding down the slide to where her mammy was waiting to catch her at the bottom. She brushed a leaf away that had fallen onto her lap. Aideen had indeed taken the blame for her over the hole in that cardigan although Una was certain Mammy had her suspicions as to what had really happened. She hadn't said a word though as she set about darning it, mending it so you'd never know it'd been there. Una knew though.

Her gaze flicked back to the house across the road. She and Aideen had always looked out for each other. It was the way it was. Until one day they hadn't. The shadow from the tree in the patch of grass out the front of the house was stretching long, signalling it was getting late in the day. Una got to her feet taking a moment to ease her aching joints which had seized from sitting too long. She'd go and see Aideen tomorrow. She definitely would, she vowed.

# Chapter 21

A isling pushed open the door of the guesthouse, holding her breath in anticipation of Marcus being sat in reception. The nervous tension must be coming off her in waves she thought. Would he be there, or wouldn't he? She was almost disappointed to see that the sofa was empty. Young Evie, looking even younger than her eighteen years with her hair pulled back in a ponytail and no make-up save for a slick of gloss, was checking a couple in. Their clothing was somewhat eccentric. The woman was in a voluminous tie-dyed dress with a long floaty cardigan overtop and a scarf draped around her neck, and he, with his silver beard and wispy long hair reminded Aisling of a wizard. Merlin sprang to mind.

Evie glanced up from the computer and caught Aisling's eye, looking as though she wanted to say something. Whatever it was would have to wait until the new arrivals had been shown to their room. Their guests always came first and, with that in mind, Aisling gathered herself, pushing thoughts of her ex aside as she came to stand alongside the bohemian pair.

'Good afternoon.' She held her hand out in greeting. It was given a warm shake in return by the gentleman. 'I'm Aisling O'Mara. Welcome to O'Mara's,' she smiled and shook his wife's hand as the gentleman introduced them both as Branok and Emblyn Nancarrow.

It was Emblyn who began to chat. She had a sing-song accent and the way in which she rolled her 'r's', made Aisling pick them as hailing from Britain's West Country. She was right. Emblyn told her they were from Falmouth in Cornwall. Privately, Aisling couldn't help but think that the Cornish had even stranger sounding names than the Irish. Emblyn and Branok? They sounded like something from *King Arthur and the Knights of the Round Table*. To be fair, he looked like something from the old Arthurian legend and he was supposed to have been born in their neck of the woods.

'And what brings you to Dublin? If you don't mind my asking?'

'Oh, I don't mind at all, dear. We're both artists. We own a gallery at home. Branok and I spent time in Dublin when we were young free spirits. Branok got it in his head that he wanted to relive his youth for a few days and visit our old haunts so,' she smiled, 'here we are.'

'It's a lot busier than I remember it,' Branok said, picking up their case, and Aisling was sure she heard him mumble, and expensive.

'When were you last here?' Aisling asked.

'Oh, sometime in the late sixties. I had even longer hair then and so did she. We spent a lot of time sitting in a semicircle in St Stephen's Green with other long-haired young people talking about the meaning of life.' He made a peace sign and Aisling and Evie laughed. 'Remember how we crashed on the floor of that communal flat at night, Emblyn?'

'I do. We'd never get up again if we did that now. The emergency services would have to be called.'

'Well now, I think you'll find your bed here much comfier than the floor. I imagine you'll find Dublin quite different on this visit, but the heart of the city is still the same.' Aisling offered to help with their case and show them to their room.

'No, we'll be fine thank you. We travel lightly. Sketch books and a few changes of clothes. Evie here has informed us of where we'll find everything we need. Now then, first floor, three doors down on the right. Come on, Emblyn, let's get settled in and then see about having a pint of Ireland's finest.'

Aisling recommended they check out Quinn's. She knew there was live music there tonight and it was only a short walk from the guest house. 'Don't hesitate to ask if you need anything. We're here to help, and have a wonderful stay,' she called after them as they trooped up the stairs.

'I'm going to head up myself, Evie. Give me a buzz if you need me.'

Evie grabbed hold of Aisling's arm before she too disappeared up the stairs startling Aisling with her vice like grip. She inclined her head toward the guest lounge, her eyes popping as she whispered, 'He's in there.'

'Who?'

'Yer man, Marcus.' Evie's voice was full of the drama of it all.

Aisling's breath caught in her throat as the thoughts raced through her head. He knew she was back, he'd have heard her voice. She'd have to go through and see him because she couldn't very well leave him sitting there. If Moira were to come home and spot him reclining on their sofa, there'd be hell to pay. For the briefest of seconds she wondered about hiding and sending Evie in to do her dirty work, but she knew that would be beyond childish.

*Be calm, be civilised, breathe slowly, and tell him to feck off,
Aisling!* she told herself licking her lips. They'd gone paper dry.
She'd not put lipstick on since finishing her lunch and her hair
had been whipped by the seafront wind. She wished Evie wasn't
sitting there because she'd have dug out her make-up purse and
tidied herself up before throwing herself into the lion's den.
She didn't want to give the younger girl gossip fodder though,
knowing she was friendly with Ita. She could just imagine what
the pair of them would say if they got their heads together. *Aisling was all concerned with looking her best! She obviously wanted
him to see what he'd missed out on. That or she wants him back.*

No, she'd been humiliated enough when he'd left and Evie,
for all that the guests thought she was marvellous, and for all
her feigned wide-eyed innocence, was quite the scandalmon-
ger. For that reason she wiped the panicked look off her face.
She took a steadying breath and thanked Evie for letting her
know in a voice that did not betray the fact her insides had jel-
lified. She held her head high and marched past the front desk
and through into the guest lounge.

# Chapter 22

There he was. Larger than life, seated in one of the wing-back chairs flicking through a magazine as though he didn't have a care in the world. His lack of interest in the magazine's content was evident in the speed with which he was flicking through the pages.

'Hello, Marcus,' she said, coming to a halt behind the sofa opposite him. His physical presence filled the room and she held onto the back of the sofa to steady herself. She'd deliberately blocked the path between them by standing where she had. There would be no cordial hello kiss. Not on her watch.

He put the magazine down on the coffee table and stood up. His smile was wide—too wide, and he looked delighted to see her. He was wearing the same Oasis shirt as yesterday she noticed wondering if he'd done so deliberately, given it had been a gift from her. A subtle reminder of happier times. Now he was at closer proximity she could see his face looked a little thinner and she watched as he rubbed at the stubble on his chin. It wasn't like him not to be clean shaven and she forced herself to meet his gaze. His hair was longer too, curling at the collar instead of the short back and sides he favoured for work. As for those swoony dark eyes, they might look tired, but they were still having that same knee weakening effect on her.

'Ash! God, it's good to see you. I hope you don't mind me waiting for you here?' He lowered his voice to a conspiratorial level. 'I couldn't face listening to Evie going on about how her trip to London to see Boyzone perform at the Party in the Park was the best thing that's ever happened to her any longer.'

She wanted to smile, but she refused to. His easy breezy way irked her. Why wasn't he on edge like she was? When she'd first met him it was this natural confidence of his that had attracted her to him. He had a practicality about him, an ability to take control of situations. His swarthy looks had whispered of a broodiness she'd wanted to tame. Those looks were deceptive she'd soon realised. Her imagination had outdone itself because Marcus worked with numbers at the bank, he was not a swashbuckling pirate. Nor did he have an intense deep side to him. What you saw was what you got with Marcus. Or at least that's what she'd thought.

She supposed with everything going on in her life when she'd moved back to Dublin, Marcus had been what she needed. Someone who'd take control and steer her down the unfamiliar path she'd found herself on because after Dad's passing, she'd been well and truly lost. Looking at him it occurred to her she didn't know what she'd expected of him—that he would have changed in the year since they parted? A grovelling apology wasn't his style. Already he'd managed to put her on the back foot which was ridiculous given he was on her territory.

'Why are you here, Marcus?' she managed to rouse herself to ask.

'You haven't replied to any of my letters.' He shrugged as though this were the obvious answer.

'Because I had nothing to say to you. You said what you wanted to say in the note you left me when you took off to Cork. You spelled things out pretty clearly.'

'Ah, Ash, that's not true. There's loads to say.'

Those eyes held hers and her heart began to beat a little too fast. She didn't want to still find him attractive. *Pretend he's Bono, Aisling.* She hummed the first few bars of Pride but the phone ringing jolted her and she lost her thread. Evie would be cursing it no doubt. She'd not be able to eavesdrop and talk on the phone, that level of multitasking wasn't in her repertoire. Aisling weakened as Marcus continued to look pleadingly at her.

'Not here.'

He glanced at his watch, 'Dinner?' then back at her hopefully.

She didn't want to sit in some cosy little restaurant listening to him blather about fresh starts. She needed to stay here on her own turf and tough it out.

'Moira's not going to be home for a while. We can talk upstairs.'

He got to his feet and Aisling turned away, not wanting him to see her face lest the thoughts she couldn't control were written all over it. He was a fine looking man alright. She used to imagine what their babies would look like. Wonder whether they would have her strawberry blonde colouring or his dark features? She'd figured they'd have his, having read somewhere that brown was the dominant gene, and that was fine by her.

Evie's eyes bored into her as she informed whoever was on the phone that they did indeed have a double room available for the twenty-first overlooking the Green. *Let her think what she likes, it's none of her business.* Aisling didn't look back as she headed up the stairs. Her spine tingled with each step, aware of Marcus's proximity to her as he followed behind.

She flicked the lights on as soon as she walked into the apartment and drew the curtains out of habit. Not once did she allow her gaze to flicker in the direction of the bedroom she'd once shared with him.

He shut the door and hovered in the entranceway seemingly not knowing where he should put himself. It must be strange to feel ill at ease in a place that had been like a second home. It was the first glimpse Aisling had had of uncertainty beneath his casual demeanour.

'It's weird being back here, Ash. If I'd handled things differently, I'd be living here with you now, as your husband.'

She wished he would stop calling her Ash. It was an intimate abbreviation, only her family and friends called her by it. His words stung. As if she needed reminding how, a year ago, her life had veered sharply off the track it had been happily tootling down. 'Well you're not and I'm going out soon. So why don't you sit down and say whatever it is you need to say.' She wasn't going anywhere, but he wasn't going to clutter her Saturday night. She pulled a chair out from the table and sat down. He did the same sitting opposite her.

She could smell him, she realised. It was the spicy musk scent she'd fallen in love with when the girl on the counter at Brown Thomas had sprayed it onto a piece of card, wafting it back and forth ceremoniously before handing it to her. She'd bought the expensive aftershave for his birthday. She wondered if he was still using the same bottle or if it had long since dried up.

Should she offer him a drink? Aisling shifted in her seat. If it were any other guest she would, but she didn't want him getting comfortable. She had no intention of making him feel at home.

'You at least read my letters?'

She nodded.

'Then there's no point in me saying I'm sorry again, you already know I am.'

The silence stretched long. Aisling feigned interest in her fingernails and Marcus cleared his throat. She wasn't going to make this easy for him.

'I was scared, Ash. It's no excuse, but it's the truth. I panicked, and I took off.'

'Why didn't you tell me how you were feeling? I would have understood.' Her voice cracked, and she hated it for letting her down.

'No you wouldn't have—don't pretend you would. I loved you. I still love you that's why I'm here. So how could I tell you I shouldn't have proposed? How was I supposed to say it was too soon to get married? I'd made a mistake because I wasn't ready—didn't know if I'd ever be ready,' he shrugged. 'I tried to convince myself it would all be okay. I was clear about how I felt about you, so we'd be grand, but you got so caught up in your plans. Each time I saw you the day was getting bigger, more elaborate. It felt like you'd forgotten what really mattered. Getting married was supposed to be about us making a commitment to each other. It terrified me, but it was a commitment I was prepared to go through with for you.'

'Stop right there.' How dare he? 'Don't you try to put the blame on me. I know what commitment is! What did you think I'd been spending all my time organising? A bloody wed-

ding so we could make that commitment! I was doing it for us.'
Was she?

'I don't mean to sound like a condescending eejit.'

'Well, you fecking do.' She was breathing heavily.

He laid both his hands down on the table palms facing up.
'What I said in the letter I left was true.'

'What? You asked me to marry you because you thought it
was what I wanted?'

'No, yes.' He shook his head. 'Kind of. I'm digging a hole
for myself. I knew I shouldn't have proposed, but it was too
late I had. So I tried to get swept up in all the plans like you
were, but somewhere along the line, it stopped being about us.
It was about the wedding. The castle, the menu, the photographer who was coming. It was all you every talked about. I
couldn't handle it.'

'Okay, so let me get this straight. Because I wanted a lovely
day, the kind of day memories are made of, like a lot of women
might I add, you thought I'd lost sight of what getting married
meant?' Aisling would have liked to throw something at him
but there was only the salt and pepper shaker within reach and
she couldn't face cleaning up the mess.

'Everything snowballed, Ash. I couldn't think clearly and
so I ran. I'm so, so sorry for leaving you to face the aftermath,
but I can't turn back time.'

'No, you can't. What's done is done and I still don't understand why you've come.'

'I want you to think about giving me another chance.'

His eyes held hers and she dropped her gaze before she lost
herself. He couldn't just walk back into her life and expect to
pick up where he'd left off.

'I get it must be a shock for you, me showing up like this and you don't have to say anything, not tonight. But know this. I love you and the biggest mistake of my life was leaving you. I'm not going to make that mistake twice. Can we try again, take things slower this time around?'

They sat in silence which Marcus broke. 'Are you happy, Ash?'

Was she? She felt like she'd been going through the motions of living since last September, nothing more.

'Please, promise me you'll think about what I've said.'

Aisling knew that now was her cue to stand up and tell him that hell would freeze over before she'd give him another chance. She should say he was a ballbag and send him packing with those bollocks of his between his knees like her mammy and sister said she should. The words, however, wouldn't come out of her mouth.

'Ash?'

'Okay.'

'You'll think about it?'

She nodded, hating herself at that moment.

'I'm staying with my mam if you want to talk or, you know, meet up. I'm in Dublin for a week.' His voice was hopeful as he got up from the table.

Aisling didn't say anything as he left closing the door behind him. She sat at that table for a long time staring at the wall but not seeing anything other than Marcus's hopeful expression as he asked if they could try again. Her mental pen began to scribble.

*Dear Aisling,*

*My ex-fiancé broke my heart. I thought I was moving on but now he says he wants me back and I'm not sure I've moved on at all. There's a part of me sorely tempted to give him a second chance because if I'm honest, I'm lonely. I think he's genuine and means what he says. Maybe we did move too fast first time around. I just don't know if I could trust him not to leave me again. My head says send him packing but my heart is wavering because I can't help but wonder if what he says about me having tunnel vision when it came to our wedding was true. What should I do? Follow my heart and see where it leads me, or my head?*

*Yours faithfully,*
*Me*

# Chapter 23

U na had dozed off early. She'd had an early and agreeable dinner at a restaurant not far from the guesthouse, Quinn's. The food was simple fare, but simple fare cooked well. At her age she couldn't be doing with spice and there seemed to be an abundance of it about these days. The Irish digestive system was not designed for the likes of chilli. It had crossed her mind to give her compliments to the chef, but she decided not to. Her clean plate was compliment enough.

She'd laid her knife and fork down as the band had begun to unpack and had been sure to settle her bill before they could so much as strike a chord. She was not in the mood for music. The maître d' had said the most peculiar thing to her as she counted out the notes from her purse. He'd said he'd known her when she was a girl, and that she and her twin sister used to love playing down by the Royal Canal. Impossible of course given he was only somewhere in the vicinity of his late thirties, but peculiar all the same and the hairs on the back of her neck had stood up.

The fresh air from her day spent observing Aideen's house had made her sleepy and she'd climbed into the double bed with its crisp white linen sheets and plump pillows in eager anticipation of a restful sleep.

She was almost grateful tonight for the now familiar rattle and clatter that stirred her from her sleep. It had dragged her from a dream where Leo was berating her; he was calling her a stubborn selfish fool of a woman. Each time she opened her mouth to ask him to stop, no sound would come out. It was most upsetting. She roused herself to peer out the curtains to the darkened courtyard below in time to spy the shadowy outline of a small creature creeping back toward the wall.

The moon came out from behind the clouds and for a moment it was as though a light had been switched on in the courtyard. She could see the fox had something in his mouth, a sausage she was fairly certain. It paused for a beat and looked up at her window. Their eyes locked and then with a flick of his tale he seemed to vanish into the wall. Una let the curtain fall and sighed.

She lay back down and watched the bedside clock, its red digits teasing her as they counted the seconds, the minutes, until finally the digits rolled over to three am. The dregs of the dream lingered like a painful hangover and she tried to focus her mind on something other than Leo's angry face. There were happy memories, lots of them, and she chose the happiest of them all.

# Chapter 24

# 1948

'I love you, Una. I have done from the moment I first saw you. You were, are the most beautiful girl I've ever seen.'

'I feel the same way. I love you too, Leo.' Una gazed adoringly into his eyes before leaning forward and planting a kiss firmly on the nose of Mr Ted, her teddy. She picked the old brown bear up; his fluffy fur had rubbed away in places from all the years of holding him close to her like she was about to do now. She hugged him tight to her chest before releasing him and pressing her index finger to her lips. She was surprised to find they were cool and dry and not on fire at the memory of Leo's lips on hers.

Leo Greene might not have said those words to her this afternoon, but he had kissed her as they meandered home alongside the banks of the canal. The weather had been overcast with a persistent light rain, the kind that eventually got its way and soaked you through to your skin. Neither of them was in a rush to get home though, and so had set their own pace despite the rain.

It was her first kiss and the butterflies it had set off in her tummy were still beating their wings madly. He'd walked her to her door and they'd coyly let go of one another's hands before saying goodbye. His hair was plastered to his forehead and her waves, that she'd spent so long taming, would now be corkscrews once more. Una had reached up and wiped away the droplet of water beginning to slide down his temple. Their eyes had locked briefly in a silent exchange that this was how it would be between them from now on, before she'd ducked inside.

She'd called out a hello before charging up the stairs two at a time. She would catch a chill if she stayed in her wet things any longer and Mam would go mad if she saw the state of her. Most of all though she wanted to relive that kiss in the privacy of her bedroom.

Leo was her and Aideen's second-best friend in the world, first place was reserved for each other. When his poor mammy died not long after he'd come to stay at his aunt's, his dad, unable to cope had asked his sister if the arrangement could be made permanent. The sisters had taken him under their wing and where they went, he went.

There'd been a subtle shift in their relationship this last year. Una had begun to see him in a different way. At sixteen he was no longer that gawky boy who was all sharp elbows and knees. He'd filled out and somewhere along the way his features had become chiselled, defining the man he was becoming. Una too had become aware of heads beginning to turn in her and Aideen's direction, of the boys, men even, eyeing them in a new manner. She hadn't returned those admiring glances. Nor to her knowledge had her sister who didn't seem to have much interest in the opposite sex. Una's reasoning was different, she only had eyes for Leo. She supposed it had been that way since they were ten years old and she'd first seen him leaning on his aunt's gate.

She'd declare all these pent-up feelings to Aideen each evening and if Aideen wasn't to hand, then Mr Ted became her confidant. Now she thought about it, Aideen had been moody of late—quieter than usual. Una shrugged thoughts of her sister aside, she was too full of the afternoon and the feel of Leo's lips on hers.

When he'd asked her to come to the cinema with him on Saturday afternoon, there was a new film people were raving about, *The Three Musketeers*. She'd declared excitedly to Aideen that this was to be a date. A proper date. She could tell in the way he had shifted nervously when he'd asked if she'd like to go. This was no wander down to the canal to look for eels!

She'd hoped he would kiss her from the moment his arm had slipped around her shoulder in the darkened theatre. The smell of damp wool hung in the air, mingling with cigarettes, and Gene Kelly and Lana Turner filled the screen in front of them. Try as she might, Una couldn't remember a single thing that happened in the film after that. All she could concentrate on was the warmth where Leo's hand rested over her shoulder. She'd moved a little closer to him and leaned her head against his shoulder like the couple in front of them.

That damp Saturday afternoon as the credits rolled down and people noisily exited the theatre chattering about the swashbuckling adventure they'd just watched, Leo had taken Una's hand. It felt natural, she'd thought, smiling up at him without guile.

It was near their old childhood haunt on the canal bank that Leo pulled her under the shelter of a tree. His face had softened as he looked at her and she'd known then that he was going to kiss her. Their lips met and began a gentle exploring dance. She didn't want him to break away, but she was frightened by where the kiss might lead if he didn't. They'd both jumped apart as though scalded as a young lad on a bike raced past, calling something cheeky that was lost on the breeze.

Una put Mr Ted down, hearing Aideen's weary footfall on the stairs. Her sister pushed the door open and kicked off her shoes. She hung her coat up and quickly changed into dry clothes, draping her damp things over the end of her bed. She'd take them downstairs to hang near the fire later. Una's wet clothes lay in a puddled heap on the floor.

Aideen flopped down on the bed. 'Ah, God, my feet are killing me.' She lifted one stockinged leg and rotated her foot in small semicircles, to the left and then to the right, before doing the same with the other leg. Aideen had started work in the ladies' wear department of Brown Thomas a month back and she was finding being on her feet all day hard work.

'I wonder if I'll get those horrible veins in my legs when I'm older like Miss Harrington. She's worked in haberdashery forever and her legs are like gnarled tree roots. No fancy stockings can hide those.' She shuddered and eyed her slender calf, her nose wrinkling at the thought. Watching her sister, Una didn't regret her decision to apply for secretarial work upon leaving school. Being employed as a typist for an accountant might not hold the glamorous allure of selling the latest fashions showcased in Brown Thomas but at least she sat down most of the day. And there was the bonus of not having to work on a Saturday!

Aideen had always hankered after employment in the grand department store. It stemmed from their annual trip to the store's sale to buy new shoes and a coat when they were smaller. Mammy was a stickler for quality and if it meant knitting and sewing everything else in her daughters' wardrobe so be it. The Brennan girls were always well-turned out—apart from when they went looking for eels, poking about by the banks of the canal!

Aideen was the quiet, dreamy sister who loved inventing stories around the lives of the well-heeled ladies with furs draped across their shoulders they'd see on those outings. She'd gawp at them swanning around the store, like gazelles at home in their natural environment. Now here she was working there, six days a week—and her feet and legs had never ached so much in her life.

It was then she saw Mr Ted and she looked from the stuffed toy to her sister noticing the silly expression she had on her face. 'What've you been doing?'

Una giggled. 'I told you I was going to see *The Three Musketeers* with Leo.'

Aideen nodded. 'Was Lana Turner gorgeous?'

'I don't know.'

Aideen's face creased in irritation, she'd had a long day and wasn't in the mood for playing silly games. 'What do you mean?'

Una giggled, oblivious to how this silly girly version of herself was annoying her sister. 'Leo put his arm around me and I don't remember much about the film at all after that. He held my hand when we walked home, and we got soaked to the bone but we didn't care. When we reached the big tree by the canal, he pulled me to him like this,' she demonstrated by picking up Mr Ted once more, 'and he kissed me.' Mr Ted bore the brunt of her affections once more and when she released him, she turned to look at her sister and said, 'Aideen it was perfect.'

~

# Present Day

U na realised she was smiling as she lay in the darkness. Her index finger was resting on her lip as it had done all those years ago when she'd sat on her bed remembering Leo's sweet kiss. Now she wondered why she hadn't noticed the way her sister's face had crumpled as she relayed the story of her and Leo's outing. How had it escaped her notice that her sister too was in love with Leo Greene and just like her had been since they were ten years old? How her disobeying her mam all those years before could have had ripples like a stone being thrown in a pond. She knew the answer. She'd had plenty of time to think on it.

It was because she hadn't wanted to see it. She was sixteen and in that way of young girls far too absorbed in her own feelings to want to acknowledge anyone else's. Her sixteen-year-old self had been caught up in the thrill of her first love, enthralled by it and she hadn't seen Aideen, not really. Una blinked away the burn of tears and sighed, partly in frustration at her lack of sleep and partly in sorrow at the way things had turned out for them.

If she were at home, she would get up and make herself a cup of tea. She listened out but there was nothing to hear, the guesthouse was silent. Would it matter if she were to go and make herself a cup of tea in the guests' lounge? It wouldn't disturb anyone, and it had to be better than lying here wide awake being tormented by things she couldn't change. Yes, she decided pushing the covers aside and sitting up, she'd make herself a cup of tea. Mammy's friend Maire had always said a good strong brew could fix anything.

# Chapter 25

Aisling's mind was whirring with thoughts of Marcus's visit and what she should do. She'd been tossing and turning for hours. This was hopeless she sighed, pulling herself upright. She flicked on the bedside light, she might as well get up and make herself a cup of tea. It would be better than spending another hour thumping her pillow in frustration.

Moira's door was open a crack and she could hear her sister snoring lightly. It had been late when she'd gotten in. Aisling had already been in bed for what felt like hours when Moira peered around her door whispering loudly, 'Ash, are you awake?' She'd stayed silent and lain still, in no mood to talk to her inebriated sister. She knew if Moira had gotten wind of Marcus having been to see her, she would be in for a tipsy tirade and the language would not be pretty. Moira gave up after a few beats and stumbled off to bed.

Aisling knew she'd be sleeping like a log so there was no need to tiptoe as she made her way through to the darkened kitchen and switched on the light. There was a slight chill in the air and she was glad of her fluffy dressing gown as she set about retrieving a mug from the dishwasher. The central heating wouldn't come on until five, timed to be toasty for the morning. It was the time of year when the early mornings and evenings were a reminder of the march of autumn toward winter.

Aisling went through the motions of filling the kettle and switching it on. She cursed under her breath as she opened the tea canister and saw it was empty. She stood there for a moment, should she forget the tea and go back to bed? The thought of lying awake until daybreak held no appeal. There were plenty of teabags in the guest lounge, she knew this because she'd restocked them again that morning.

Should she brave going downstairs? No one would be about at this time. She wouldn't disturb anyone, not if she was quiet. Her decision made, she went and searched out her slippers and, being careful not to lock the apartment door behind her—she'd have to set off the fire alarms if she locked herself out and needed to wake Moira—she set off down the stairs. Every creak of the old timber beneath the carpet seemed magnified in the silence of the old house and she stood cringing for a second or two on the staircase before taking the next step.

She finally reached the bottom and stood frozen by the realisation that a light was on in the lounge. The door was pulled to but not shut, and in the darkness she could see the glimmer creeping out through the cracks. It wasn't like Evie to forget to turn everything off. Her dad picked her up faithfully at ten pm and she always did the rounds before locking up for the night of a weekend.

Who would be sitting in there at this hour of the night? Perhaps one of their guests had had one too many and fallen asleep on the sofa. She'd take a peek. It wouldn't be fair for James to be confronted by some drunkard when he arrived in the morning—that was not in his job description!

Aisling pushed the door open and peered into the room, blinking against the sudden brightness. It took her a second to realise Una Brennan was staring back at her. She was sitting in one of the antique wingback armchairs. A small figure shrouded in her dressing gown which was green like the fabric Mammy had chosen to recover the chairs in. *To tie the curtains in and bring the whole look together,* she'd said. A cup of tea was cooling on the teak occasional table and the light came not from the chandelier dangling from the middle of the ceiling, but rather the freestanding reading lamp. It illuminated Miss Brennan somewhat spookily from behind.

Una's eyes mirrored the same surprise as Aisling's, cats' eyes caught in headlights at finding one another awake at this time.

Aisling spoke first. 'I'm sorry to disturb you, Miss Brennan,' she stepped into the room. 'I've run out of teabags upstairs. I'll just grab a couple and leave you in peace.' She'd given the woman a fright she knew, but then she'd gotten one herself.

'You couldn't sleep either?' Una asked, her heart beginning to slow to its normal rate of beats per minute once more. She hadn't known who was going to appear when the door had squeaked open and she was acutely aware that she was in her robe and slippers.

'No, things on my mind and the harder I try not to think about them the worst it gets.' Aisling smiled ruefully making her way over to the buffet to retrieve the teabags.

'I'd like the company if you care to join me.' Una was surprised at the words that popped unbidden from her mouth.

Aisling too was taken aback. This was not the same shrewish woman she'd been encountering these last few mornings.

'Thank you. I'll make myself a cuppa, would you like a top up?'

'Yes ta.'

Aisling set about making the tea all the while wondering over the peculiar situation she found herself in.

'My mam had a friend who always said a cuppa could fix anything.' Una repeated her earlier sentiment out loud this time as Aisling placed the cup and saucer down next to her and picking up her own cup sat down in the chair on the other side of the occasional table.

Aisling blew on the steam rising from her teacup. 'I don't think a cup of tea is going to fix my problem.'

'Nor mine,' Una said. 'When I was little I used to think tea must have magical properties if it could fix things.'

Aisling raised a smile. 'My mammy always says that a problem shared is a problem halved.' It was one of Maureen O'Mara's favourite sayings.

'Hmm, simplistic but possibly more helpful than tea alone.'

Aisling stole a glance at the older woman, her face looked gentler than it had this morning. She realised it was because she wasn't wearing the disgruntled expression she'd perpetually had in place since arriving at O'Mara's. It would be nice to confide in someone who could view her situation from a neutral vantage point.

'You could be my Switzerland,' she said.

'I beg your pardon?'

'Oh, sorry, I was thinking aloud. What I meant was that if I talk to you, you'd be neutral. You won't have a pre-existing opinion like my family and friends. They all think my ex, Marcus is a selfish eejit.'

'Ah, I see.'

They sat in silence for a minute or two sipping their respective tea. It was Aisling who spoke up.

'This time last year we were going to be married. We hadn't known each other long, but I knew as soon as I met him, he was the one for me. Or, at least I thought I did.' Aisling began haltingly at first and then decided, as her mammy would say, in for a penny in for a pound.

'He wasn't, because he took off for Cork two weeks before our wedding with a bad case of cold feet. All he left behind was a note saying he loved me, but he didn't want to marry me. I was beside myself, but I threw myself into managing this place and I was beginning to see that my life would go on without him when he started writing to me. He'd made a mistake and he wanted me back. I ignored his letters, but they kept coming and then yesterday he came here, to the guesthouse to see me. I wanted to hate him or at the very least still be angry with him and I tried as hard as I could to conjure up those emotions, but I couldn't.'

'And now part of you wants to give him a second chance and part of you feels that to do so would be letting yourself down.'

'Exactly.' Aisling drained her tea. 'Listening to him yesterday it became clear why he never wanted to get married. His parents have an unhappy life together and he's scared of winding up like them. He got caught up in the idea of it because he says, *it's what he thought I wanted.*'

'And did you?'

She nodded. 'My dad hadn't long passed, and I was pleased to have something else to focus on. So yes, I suppose I got swept up in the idea of a perfect day but now, I'm not sure now whether it was for Marcus and me at all. I've had plenty of time to think and I can see I was using the wedding as an antidote for me, Mammy, Roisin, and Moira to Dad dying. Only there is no antidote to grief. We were all reeling from his illness and the fact he wasn't with us anymore when I met Marcus. I think that's why our relationship moved as fast as it did. Maybe I did bully him along. Oh, I don't know.' Aisling shrugged. 'What he did leaving the way he did, I just don't know if I can ever move past that.'

'Yes, I can quite see your problem.' Una took a sip of her tea as she mulled over Aisling's predicament. 'The solution's really rather simple though.'

It was? This was promising. Aisling leaned toward Una eager to hear what she would say next.

'You must follow your heart, dear. There's a lot to be said for forgiveness, Aisling. It isn't always an easy thing to do, but it is the right thing to do. You don't want to live a life of regrets because you were too proud to find a way back.'

Aisling got the distinct impression they were no longer talking just about her and Marcus.

'I was engaged once too. A long time ago now.' Una's voice snagged as she found herself wheeling back in time to 1950, telling Aisling the story of that year and how what had happened had changed the course of her life irrevocably.

# Chapter 26
# 1950

Una pushed open the front gate and made her way up the path. She'd finished work early having asked Mr Hart if she might go home. She'd woken that morning feeling odd and as the day had stretched on, she'd begun to feel decidedly unwell. The contents of her breakfast had been tossed up in the toilet and her throat was hot and aching. Her eyes were burning, and she couldn't focus on the paperwork she was supposed to be typing. She was chilled one minute and fiery the next. A pink rash too had appeared in the creases of her arms. It alarmed her, and she'd desperately tried not to scratch at it.

A bout of flu no doubt, Mr Hart had tutted, his tone suggesting she shouldn't have come in to the office at all spreading her germs. He sent her home. She'd sat with her aching head resting against the window of the bus as it wound its way through the streets to the stop closest to home. She could do without getting sick. Her plan had been to race down to Dawson Street on her lunch break to pick up the copy of Modern Bride she'd ordered in. It was due to arrive today. Mammy had offered to sew her wedding dress and she wanted to get some ideas as to the latest styles.

The wedding dress could wait, and she shut her eyes briefly, willing the bus to hurry up. All she wanted was to sleep.

How she made it up the stairs to her bed was a blur. So too were the events that transpired from then until her fever broke and she found herself in a hospital bed. She was in a ward with only one other bed. It was occupied by a young girl of about six or seven years who hailed from a small village in County Clare. She was tucked up in the bed across from Una. Her large eyes in her head showed she was very poorly. It was a mystery to Una as to what she was doing there.

It was explained by one of the kindlier nurses, her voice muffled by the mask she wore, she had scarlet fever and was to stay in the Cork Fever Hospital in isolation for the next three to four weeks at least. Where she'd caught the illness was a mystery.

Her only visitors during that time were her mam and her dad. They came once a week but even they were not allowed in to see her. They could merely stand at the glass and tell her the news. Mam told her they'd burned her bedding on the advice of the doctor who'd made the diagnosis before she was whisked away in the ambulance. Neither they nor Aideen were showing any symptoms, thank the lord. Leo too was fighting fit. They sent their love.

Una was grateful for those visits. They were her only link with the outside world. Her world consisted of hushed, no-nonsense voices, an all-pervasive smell of carbolic soap, and scratchy sheets. She knew too her mam would struggle bringing herself to the less than salubrious part of the city where the hospital was located. This wasn't out of snobbery but rather fear. Fear of catching something like the dreaded tuberculosis which was raging through the city. The rest of the wards in the hospital would have been full of people afflicted with the illness.

It was such a strange time, she was sick, yes, but still lucid enough to be lonely, homesick, and terribly bored. What it must have been like for the little girl who shared the small space with her Una couldn't comprehend. To be so little and so far away from home must have been terrifying. The nurse had confided that the girl, Maggie, had rheumatoid fever on top of the scarlet fever and would be staying longer than Una. If indeed Maggie had felt frightened by the alien space, she found herself in she never said. In fact, she barely strung a sentence together the whole time Una was there despite their proximity.

With nothing else in which to occupy her time, Leo filled her thoughts. It was a form of torture not to be able to see him and she missed Aideen terribly, even if she had been a moody mare this last while. She'd felt a distance growing between her and her sister over the course of the year. Una put it down to the difference in their circumstances. She was a young woman with a fiancé while Aideen, despite several advances had declined all her potential suitors. She was too picky by far and if she weren't careful, she'd wind up an old spinster Una would think, plucking at her sheets in irritation.

She thought it likely, although she'd never ask and Aideen would never say, that she was envious of her situation. She was jealous of the way in which Leo took up so much of her time these days. It was time previously reserved for each other and of course Leo too had been as much a part of Aideen's world as he had Una's, from the time they were ten years old. The old saying three's a crowd was true, however. One couldn't conduct a romance with a third party in tow. Perhaps her sister had felt pushed out. She put herself in her sister's shoes and decided that this must be the case.

She'd been so caught up in her own love affair she hadn't spared the time to think about Aideen and how it must have affected her. She'd merely found her twin's moodiness a selfish irritant designed to dampen her own happiness.

It was the way of life though wasn't it? Things had to change, people grew up and fell in love. They got married and started families of their own. She made up her mind that she would talk to Aideen once she was well and home once more, to explain all of this to her. Tell her that just because she was going to start a new chapter with Leo didn't mean that there wouldn't always be a special place reserved for Aideen. They were part of each other after all. Two halves that made a whole.

Yes, she resolved, she would smooth the waters over once she got home.

In between these musings she'd lie on her bed fed up with herself and her bland surroundings. She'd imagine where Leo was and what he'd be doing at different times during the day. Her mind would drift toward their wedding. No date had been set but still she'd imagine herself in a dress similar to that worn by Elizabeth Taylor in her May wedding to Conrad Hilton Jr. Aideen as bridesmaid would wear blue, it was her favourite colour. She'd get swept along in a tide of images depicting horse-drawn carriages and magnificent cathedrals where she and Leo would exchange vows.

She was not delusional though; she and Leo were not royalty or Hollywood stars and the reality was her dress would be handmade by her mother. It would not be as voluminous as Elizabeth Taylor's shimmery, satin affair but it would be pretty. The gown would be made with the sort of love money could never buy and she would feel every inch the beautiful bride. The ceremony would take place in St Peter's Church where they had attended Mass for as long as they'd resided in Phibsborough—forever! As for her carriage, she had her fingers crossed Dad would be able to borrow his boss's Bentley to drive her and Aideen to the church.

A honeymoon would be nice too. Una hadn't seen much of life outside of Dublin. She didn't think the odd stay down at her cousin Janet's near Wexford counted for much. Connemara would be pretty; she'd seen pictures of it in springtime in a magazine when the purple heather had formed a glorious carpet around the lakes. Or if they saved enough money, they could cross the water and visit Wales; she had a second cousin who lived on a farm there.

Una would flush as she thought about what her nights might be like on her honeymoon. The lovemaking was something she didn't know much about. She and Aideen had gleaned what little information they did have from the whispered conversations of girls at school. It was something she suspected that while initially a little frightening would ultimately be something she'd enjoy very much—if those yearnings she felt when she and Leo kissed were anything to go by!

The time passed as time does, and the day came when Una left that white-walled hospital room. She felt sad to be leaving little Maggie on her own but she couldn't wait to escape the confines and she didn't look back as she walked away from the building. Her dad picked her up in his new Anglia. This was something that had changed in the time she'd been in hospital.

The family now had a car. It made Una aware that while she had been shut away life had indeed gone on.

The car was her dad's pride and joy and he gave her a running commentary of the mechanics behind it as they pootled home. Mam he mentioned, in between explaining how the gears worked, had organised a party tea. A celebration of their girl being well and coming home. Una walked through their front door already tired from the exertions of leaving the hospital and listening to her dad. She was pale and thin and felt like she'd been away for months, not weeks, but she was home.

She was greeted warmly and if things were off with Aideen and Leo, she didn't pick up on it. She never saw her mammy's worried frown as she glanced from each of her daughters and back over to Leo. Nor did she hear the forced joviality in her dad's voice as he tried to ward off the storm he knew was coming. The illness had left her drained, and oblivious to the shifting sands of their relationship. They'd been sifted through and redefined while she'd been in hospital. But she knew nothing of this.

# Chapter 27

# Present Day

The clatter of Aisling's teaspoon against her saucer as she placed her cup back down startled Una from her story. It was jarring in the silence, a quiet only broken by Una's murmuring voice. 'Do you know, even thinking about my spell in hospital conjures up the smell of carbolic soap. I couldn't get the stench of it from my nostrils for the longest time.'

Aisling stared into her empty teacup, there were no tea leaves at the bottom and she didn't believe in that sort of thing, anyway. Nevertheless, she had a fair idea what was coming. She was so caught up in the emotion of what she'd been listening to, she hadn't been aware of her eyes beginning to smart with unshed tears at the unfairness of Una's story. She blinked hard to ward them off.

'Leo and Aisling waited until I was back to full health before they said anything.'

It was no good the blinking didn't work, and a tear rolled down Aisling's cheek, it was as she'd feared. She swiped it away feeling a surge of anger for this woman, a virtual stranger whose life she now knew intimately, at the events that had unfurled fifty years ago.

'It was Leo who told me it was Aideen he'd loved all along. He called for me a week or so after I got home. The fresh air would do me good he said suggesting a stroll alongside the canal. It must have been a Saturday because Aideen wasn't home. I can remember seeing Mam's face, pale and anxious as she told me to be sure to do my coat up. I put it down to her worrying about my health, but I think she had an inkling that things weren't as they'd been between Leo and me. There was a tension between us as we set off. A sudden awareness on my part that something had changed between us over the course of my hospital stay. I wondered why he didn't reach for my hand like he always did but I didn't say anything. When he suggested we sit down on a bench not far from the spot where we'd shared that first kiss, I was grateful for the opportunity to rest. The short walk had left me breathless and my limbs felt like dead weights. I'd been told to expect this; it would be a long time before my physical health returned to what it had been. It wasn't just my physical self that had been damaged though, my brain too seemed to struggle to process things for a long time after I left the hospital. I couldn't hold onto thoughts for any length of time. Words I wanted to say would be right there and then they'd dissipate like smoke. Such a strange time.' She shook her head and toyed with the tie of her dressing gown for a beat before continuing.

'Once I was settled on the seat, Leo took my hand and I felt a weight lift because I thought to myself that everything would be alright now. It was then he explained in a matter-of-fact manner he'd made a mistake. His voice was steady, measured, as though he'd practised what he was going to say to me. I couldn't make sense of it. This wasn't the Leo I knew, and I thought it must be me not processing things properly. I'd misunderstood because his words were nonsensical. Him and Aideen? It only sank in when he took his hand away from mine. This was how things would be from now on. It would be my sister's hand, not mine he'd be holding.'

'Oh, Una!' Aisling got up and put her cup and saucer down on the buffet. She wanted to hug the older woman, but Una held her hand up to silence her. She needed to finish, she needed to share this story. She'd never breathed a word of it to anyone since the day Leo Greene had shattered her heart into pieces so small she'd never managed to put them back together again.

'It was my personality you see. I didn't understand what he meant, and he tried to explain saying I was so strong-willed. He'd gotten swept along by the sheer force of what I wanted. It was only when I was convalescing that he'd had time to clear his head and think properly, to understand his feelings. It had been Aideen all along. Quiet gentle Aideen. I don't remember much of what he said after that. They were words that tumbled on top of each other rather like clothes in a washing machine. What needed to be said had been said and the rest was just that, words. It had become clear that Aideen too had been in love with him just as I had from the time she was ten years old. I'd chosen not to see it because then my feelings for Leo would have been impossible. I was hurt, yes, and I might have been able to move on from the pain eventually, but not the humiliation. That and the sense of betrayal was the worst of it, Aisling. I was a proud woman, foolishly proud.'

'I know a little about what that's like,' Aisling murmured, her heart going out to this woman huddled inside her dressing gown on the chair next to her. Her story was far more wounding than Aisling's, she'd been hurt by the two people she was closest to in the whole world. Heartbreak was heartbreak though and she did know how deep that pain cut. Her words had echoed those of Marcus too, he'd said he'd gotten swept along by what she wanted.

Una nodded. 'Yes, I suppose you do.'

Aisling got up and took the cup and saucer from Una's whose hand was shaking. She placed it on the buffet next to her own before sitting back down. Una began talking again. 'I couldn't get the thoughts out of my head of how I'd prattled on about the wedding to them both. How I'd told them it was all I thought about while I was in the hospital and all the while they'd nodded and smiled, told me how good it was I well again. How great it was I was home. All that time they'd known my talk of getting married was farcical. How could Aideen, whom I'd confided all my hopes and dreams in do that to me? It ate away at me for the longest time.'

'What did you do, you know, after Leo told you how he felt?'

'It was a little like being sick again, there are chunks of time I can't recall but I do remember shouting at Aideen and grabbing at her hair; where that strength came from, I don't know. Mam pulled me off her. It was Aideen who bore the brunt of my anger. I couldn't carry on living under the same roof as her and so I packed my bags. Mam and Da begged me to stay. Time would heal Mam said, but I wouldn't listen. I only made one stop after I left the house that day and that was to Mr Hart. I thanked him for his kindness in holding my job open while I was ill and for allowing me the extra time to recuperate at home, but I wouldn't be coming back.' Una's laugh held no mirth. 'Oh, the look on his studious face when I told him I was leaving due to the fact my sister; my twin sister no less, had stolen my fiancé. Thus rendering my life in Dublin intolerable.'

Such was the picture Una was painting Aisling could almost see the small middle-aged man with thinning hair sitting behind his desk. The scandalised expression he'd have worn at what his young secretary was telling him.

'I took all the money Leo and I'd saved for our wedding out of the bank and closed the account. There was no guilt in the act, I felt I was owed it after what he'd done. I said goodbye to Mr Hart and made my way to the train station. I boarded the first train out of Dublin. I didn't care where I wound up so long as it was miles away from the city.'

'And you wound up in Waterford.'

'Yes. I made a new life for myself there.'

'But what about your mam and dad?'

'I think I regret the pain I caused them the most. My poor dad somewhat ironically was killed in an accident in his beloved Anglia not long after I left. But something had happened to me in the aftermath of Leo and Aideen. It was like my heart had been hardened. I couldn't feel like I felt before. It was like nothing would ever cut quite so deep again. I wrote to Mammy and told her where I was. She came to visit me but things between us were always strained because of my refusal to hear any news about my sister. I would not and could not forgive her or Leo.'

'And you never saw either of them again?'

'I saw them twice, both times at funerals, first Dad's and then Mam's. I kept my distance from them and their sons both times; they had three boys all close in age. Aideen tried to make amends, she wrote and asked to be forgiven but I couldn't get past what had happened. Leo tried to put things right, he approached me after Mam's service, but I gave him short shrift. He got rather angry and called me a selfish woman.'

It was unfair of Leo, Aisling mused because she could see how hard it would be to mend bridges that had been blown to smithereens. But it also seemed, listening to her tale, that despite the wrongs done to her it was Una who'd lost out in the end. Her life had never been whole since she left Dublin because of her refusal to bend in her emotions. She'd lost not just her fiancé, she'd lost her family too. It was just too sad. She swiped another rogue tear away with the back of her hand.

Una glanced at her sharply. 'Don't waste your tears on me, Aisling. What's done is done. It was my foolish fault not to at least try to find some forgiveness in my heart. If I had I might have been able to open myself up to the possibility of someone else, but I was too stubborn for that and I'd lost the ability to trust in others.'

'You never met anyone else?'

'Oh, I had a few suitors over the years, but I wouldn't let them close enough to hurt me. One by one they got tired of being held at arm's length and moved on.' Una reached over then and took hold of Aisling's hand giving it a brief squeeze. 'Don't let pride stand in the way of happiness, my dear. If you're sure of your feelings and you still love this man, then find a way to put that wedding business behind you and give him another chance.'

Aisling shifted uncomfortably. She didn't know how she felt. Marcus's sudden appearance had her in a spin. She did know she was scared of making the wrong choice and regretting it in years to come. She didn't want to be like Una living a life in bitterness. She deflected the subject from herself, curious as to why Una had come back to Dublin now, after all those years. What had changed? 'Why are you here now?'

Una didn't answer the question right away, she still seemed lost in the past. 'Do you know I used to walk past O'Mara's on my way to work for Mr Hart?' It wasn't a question rather a statement and a small smile played at the corners of her mouth. 'I dreamed of what it would be like behind the grand brick facade and I used to imagine the stories that had played out inside these walls. It's funny to think my story's part of the fretwork now too isn't it?'

Aisling smiled gently. 'Una, I hope your story's going to have a happy ending.'

'You asked me, why I've come back?'

Aisling nodded.

'Aideen wrote to me not long ago. It was the first letter I'd received from her in years. She'd long since given up on contacting me and I suppose I was curious as to why she was getting in touch after all this time. I felt compelled to read it and once I had, well I had no choice but to come back.'

Aisling was on the edge of the seat.

'Leo passed a few years back, a heart attack. It was a terrible shock by all accounts. No warning. One minute he was standing in the kitchen talking to her about the early peas in the garden, the next he'd keeled over and that was that. It's strange to imagine him gone. To know I'll never see him again. I suppose I always thought I might one day, that somehow, we'd all come back together, but time marches on. That wasn't what she wrote to tell me though. She wrote to say she's sick herself. It's breast cancer.'

'Oh, I'm sorry, is she having treatment? What's her prognosis?' She might never have met Una's twin, but she felt now as though she had, privy as she'd been to the sisters' past.

'She didn't get into any of that. She didn't write so as I'd feel sorry for her or anything like that. She got in touch because she wanted to tell me to go and get checked myself.'

'You should, Una, things like that can be hereditary and if it's caught quick enough, well the doctors can work wonders these days.' She shivered thinking of her own dad's fight with stomach cancer. It was still an open wound. She knew he'd been unwell for a long time before he'd gone to the doctor. He'd always had an aversion to medical practitioners. There was no reason for this so far as Aisling knew, other than he thought he knew better. A glass of Guinness could fix anything. *Sure*, he'd say, *the black stuff is a meal in a glass. It's loaded with goodies.*

Aisling couldn't help but wonder if he hadn't been so pigheaded whether his cancer might have been caught sooner. Things may have had a different outcome.

She knew right enough that the disease was hard to detect in the early stages. She'd heard all the jargon, but they'd never know for sure whether it might have been picked up had he been checked. She'd never voiced these thoughts out loud and she didn't know if anyone else in the family shared her sentiment. It would be pointless to bring it up now, achieving nothing because he was gone and, as Una had just said, that was that.

'I started thinking after I read her letter and I couldn't stop thinking about what Aideen was like when we were young. She looked out for me. I was the wilful one who skirted the edges of trouble, but she always had my back.'

Her eyes, Aisling saw, were glazed with faraway memories of the past.

'There was an occasion I couldn't get out of my head. It was the day we met Leo for the first time and I insisted on wearing my new cardigan despite Mam specifically telling me not to—not when looking for eels. She'd knitted identical blue cardigans with the prettiest of flower trims for Aideen and me. I knew I should do as I was told but I didn't. I wore it because I wanted to impress him, even then there was something about Leo Greene. Somehow as we were getting up to go home Leo's stick got snagged in it and when he freed it, there was a gaping hole. He told me the day he broke it off between us, he'd felt so terribly bad all those years ago about that. There he'd been homesick and missing his mam, going to the canal with Aideen and I was the tonic he'd needed. He said he'd been grateful I'd taken the time to talk to him, and then he'd gone and spoiled it. He'd been making it up to me ever since.' Una shook her head. 'Fancy him feeling like that, I had no idea. At the time it happened I was sick to my stomach because it meant I'd miss out on our annual trip to the zoo. Aideen said she didn't want to go without me and took the cardigan from me, wearing it home herself. She told Mam it was hers and that she'd been showing off to the lad who'd come to stay with Mrs Greene down the road. I don't think Mam believed her—she knew me too well—but she had no choice and you see that's the way Aideen was. She wasn't cruel and spiteful or selfish as I tried to convince myself. The enormity of all these lost years hit me then.' Una's voice cracked for the first time. 'So, that's why I came back.'

Aisling got up and put her arm around her shoulder. They stayed like that for a few minutes and she couldn't help but think what an incongruous sight the pair of them made in their nightwear spilling their secrets in the dead of the night.

'Have you been to see Aideen, Una?' Aisling asked assuming that this was where the woman had gone each day since she'd come to stay at the guesthouse.

'No, not exactly.'

Aisling was puzzled. 'But I thought that was why you'd come to Dublin?'

'It is, and I've caught a taxi to the street where she lives every day since I arrived, but I haven't been able to walk up her front path and knock on her door. I've been sitting across the street on a bench in the park opposite.'

It was a good job the weather had behaved itself, Aisling thought. Then again, maybe if the heavens had opened Una might have been forced to shelter inside Aideen's house.

'I don't know how I'll be received you see. She never asked me to come back. She might hate me, Aisling. She might be angry with me for leaving and not trying to work things out. She might think me a selfish old fool, and I have been.' Una's voice rose several notches and she looked small and vulnerable, absolutely nothing like the cantankerous woman Aisling had encountered each morning.

'I don't think so, Una. You said she was your other half.'

Una nodded.

'Well, I think you'll find she understands why you couldn't stay. You were hurt badly by her and Leo, what they did, even if it was done out of love for each other and not with the intent of hurting you, is not something most people would find easy to forgive.'

Una wasn't listening. 'I've come to realise I'm a coward. I ran away when I couldn't face what had happened and now, I can't summon the courage to knock on my own twin's door.'

Aisling didn't need to compose one of her letters, the answer was simple. 'You're not a coward, Una! I think you're very brave for coming here. You've just got to take the next step. Do you think it would help if we went to Aideen's house together?'

Una looked at the pretty young woman opposite her. That glorious red blonde hair of hers was sticking up here, there, and everywhere, the result of all the tossing and turning she must have done before making her way downstairs. 'You'd do that for me?'

'I would gladly come with you but I'm afraid you're going to have to do something for me in return first.'

Una felt her guard go up. She should have known there was nothing for nothing in this life.

'I want you to tell Mrs Flaherty how much you enjoy her white pudding. She's a little temperamental our cook, and a little praise goes a long way with her. It's her day off tomorrow but she'll be back on board Monday morning and it would get the week off to a good start!'

Una looked at Aisling in disbelief and her lips curved into a smile, mirroring the girl opposite her. 'I think I can do that.'

# Chapter 28

O n Sunday morning the run of good weather decided it had had enough and when Aisling woke, she could hear the rain pelting against her bedroom window. The sound of it hitting the panes of glass was something she'd always loved. To lie in bed, warm and cosy, knowing outside was cold and wet, was a snuggly treat and she burrowed down under her covers.

Marcus's handsome features floated in front of her and she conjured up the warmth of his body and the way in which he used to press himself up against her. She could almost feel his breath on her neck and the tingles it would send up and down her spine. They'd fitted together, slotted into place like pieces in a jigsaw puzzle.

*He's a selfish eejit. A spoiled only child used to getting his own way and when he doesn't, he throws his toys out of the cot.* Moira's words reverberated in her ear. Would he flounce off to another city the next time he felt she didn't have his best interests at heart? People did make mistakes though. Listening to Una's sad story last night had opened her eyes to that. Nobody was perfect, but did people change?

The birds had been chirping by the time she and Una had made their way back to their beds, exhausted and spent. Neither woman had any wish to be caught out in their nightwear by an early-rising guest so they'd said goodnight or good morning, unsure what was appropriate. They'd arranged to meet in the guest lounge once more. This time however it would be at the respectable hour of eleven am, and with that, they'd hugged each other tightly. Aisling had climbed the stairs, let herself quietly back into the apartment and fallen into bed, drifting off into a dreamless sleep almost straight away.

It was quite amazing, she thought, enjoying the weight of her bedding on her that she should form such a strong bond in such a short space of time with a woman she'd dreaded bumping into these last few mornings! Who would have thought?

Still waters run deep she mused, then realising that was exactly the sort of thing Mammy would say changed the sentiment to you could never judge a book by its cover. That was worse! She decided to abandon the train of thought and risk a peek at the clock. It was nine forty-five and she felt a stab of guilt at having lain in so late.

Normally she would have been up and about making sure O'Mara's morning routines were playing out as they should be. The guesthouse under her watch ran like a well-oiled machine or at least she liked to think it did; Ita's face floated to mind—the exception to the rule. Still, she was off today, and it would be Geraldine humming as she stripped beds and vacuumed.

It was a pity Geraldine and Ita didn't swap places. Geraldine had no interest in working more than the four hours she did of a Sunday morning though. Not with three littlies running around at home. Her Sunday morning job, she'd confided in Aisling, was a welcome break from the routines of being Mam to her trio, but by the time one o'clock rolled around she was ready for the off, eager to see them all again.

James would have been stationed at the front desk for well over an hour now too, Aisling knew. He'd have already demolished the enormous plate of eggs, bacon, and sausage Mrs Baicu foisted on to him every Sunday morning not long after he let himself in. She had sons herself she said and knew how much they loved to eat. She'd come to Ireland with her husband from Romania many moons ago and would be in the kitchen cooking up a storm. Her roots might not hail from here, but she could still whip up a full Irish fry-up to rival Mrs Flaherty's with her eyes closed. Not that Aisling would ever tell Mrs Flaherty that!

They were all more than capable of doing their jobs without Aisling peering over their shoulders. And while they might wonder where she was this morning, O'Mara's would not grind to a halt without her. Nevertheless, it was time she got up if she were going to be ready in time to meet Una. She needed a strong cup of coffee after her broken night.

She hoped Una had managed to catch a few hours solid sleep too. She'd need it. They had a big afternoon planned. This time Una would walk up the front path and knock on Aideen's door. She tossed her blankets aside and shrugging into her dressing gown and slippers once more padded through to the kitchen.

Moira was already up. Her dark hair was tied back in a loose ponytail and she was lounging on the sofa in her pyjamas, the television tuned into a soap opera where everybody on the screen looked hard done by. She was engrossed in their problems and didn't hear Aisling enter the room as she spooned cereal into her mouth.

'Good night was it?' Aisling called as she set about making herself a cup of coffee. 'You were snoring like a train. I could hear you through the walls.' At least she was up and about and looking a lot brighter than she had yesterday morning, she thought as she retrieved the coffee jar.

'I don't snore and yes it was a good craic, we met up with some friends and carried on until late. Copper Face Jack's was going off,' Moira mumbled through the sugary frosted flakes she insisted on buying. 'Oh, before I forget Roisin rang earlier. Mammy's been on to her with the breaking news Marcus feck-ing coward McDonagh's sniffing around. Anyway, she said she'll ring back just after ten. How come you're not downstairs telling everybody how to do their jobs?'

'I fancied a lie in for a change.'

'You haven't got anyone in there have you?' Moira put her spoon down and turned her narrowed eyes in her sister's direc-tion.

'No!'

'Just as well, because if you did then I'd have no choice but to ring Mammy and tell her you had Marcus fecking coward McDonagh holed up in your bedroom. Then you'd be for it.'

'Ha-ha.' Actually, it wasn't funny, the wrath of Maureen O'Mara, if she had indeed spent the night with her ex, would not be a pleasant thing to bear witness to at all. She sighed, it was clear, even if she decided to give Marcus another chance—perhaps take things slower this time around without the pressure of a big white wedding looming—her family weren't going to let him off the hook lightly.

Aisling poured the boiling water into her cup, stirring it as she debated confiding in Moira. She wouldn't tell her about her conversation with Una last night. That was between the two of them, but she decided she might as well own up to Marcus having been here where she got back yesterday. If she didn't,

Moira would hear it through the O'Mara's grapevine anyway and be suspicious as to why Aisling hadn't said anything. 'Marcus called around yesterday.'

The cereal bowl was placed down on the coffee table and the television muted as Moira swivelled around to stare at her sister; she was all ears.

'And?'

'He wants us to put the wedding business behind us and start again.'

The noise Moira emitted would have been more at home in a farmyard than in the apartment of a Georgian manor house.

'Charming,' Aisling muttered taking a much-needed swig of her coffee.

'What did you say? I hope it began with an 'f' and was followed by an off.'

'No, not exactly.'

'Ash!'

Aisling banged her cup down on the bench sending a slop of the brown brew over the side of her mug. 'He's genuinely sorry, Moira! Not everything's black and white in life, sometimes there are shades in between. It's alright for you. You're twenty-five, you've got plenty of time left to make mistakes and meet Mr Right. I'm nearly thirty-five and I wanted to settle down and hopefully start a family in the not too distant future. What if Marcus was the 'one'? What if I send him packing once and for all and down the line realise it was the worst mistake of my life?'

'He's not.'

'How do you know?'

'Because the 'one' would never do what he did to you and the worst mistake of your life would be taking him back. What would Mammy say?'

'I don't know!'

'Yes, you do.'

'Don't.'

'Do too.'

Aisling knew she wasn't going to win. 'A leopard doesn't change his bloody spots,' she muttered.

'Exactly and Mammy'd be right. You get back with him, Ash, and somewhere down the line when the going gets tough he'll leave you in the lurch again. Only this time around you might have a couple of kiddies to worry about too.'

The sisters glared at each other and the phone ringing was a welcome diversion. Aisling pounced on it.

'It's me. You're up.'

Aisling rolled her eyes, she'd forgotten Roisin was calling back. She'd had more than enough familial lecturing for one day as it was without her bossy older sister getting on the bandwagon. She sighed down the line, 'Hi, Rosie, how're ya keepin?'

'Grand here. You could at least sound pleased to hear from me though, Ash.'

'She's all mardy because she's had feck face around!' Moira shouted from the sofa. Aisling wasn't quick enough to cover the receiver.

'You never!'

'She did!'

'Shut up, Moira.' Aisling hissed carrying the phone out of the room and into the privacy of her bedroom. She pushed the door shut with her foot before flopping down on her bed.

'He was here when I got back from lunch with Mammy yesterday, Rosie. I didn't ask him to come.'

'Mammy says he's been writing to you for months. You kept that quiet. Noah go and do some colouring or something. You can have a word in a minute, I'm talking to Aunty Aisling first.'

'Because I knew what you'd all say that's why.' Aisling caught sight of herself in the dressing table mirror and grimaced. Her eyes were like two pee holes in the snow. She was in desperate need of mascara and getting up she rummaged through her cosmetic purse sitting beneath the mirror.

'You can hardly blame us, Ash. We saw the state you were in when he left. It was us who had to pick up the pieces. I tell you he's got some nerve thinking he can waltz back in to your life. Mammy says he wants you to give him another chance.'

The O'Mara women's bush telegraph was in fine fettle it would seem, Aisling retrieved her tube of Lustrous Lash.

'He does, and I think he means what he says, he made a mistake. We're all only human, Rosie, and he felt like he was being steamrollered by me where the wedding was concerned.'

'Bully for him. Colin had to deal with Mammy hijacking ours, but he still stuck around and said I do. You remember, Ash, the poor man had to watch me walking down the aisle looking like I was wearing one of those crochet toilet-roll cover dresses Nanna Dee used to make. She crocheted eleven of the bloody things, one for us and one for every loo in the guest house. Mammy would only put them out when she came to stay. Ugh, they used to give me the willies, horrible doll eyes staring at me while I was sat on the throne.'

Rosie was easily side-tracked so Aisling got back on the subject. 'No, you don't get it. I've been thinking about it a lot and I did turn into bridezilla. It was only because I was so determined to give us all a day to remember, a happy day after everything we'd been through with Dad. I wish Marcus had tried talking to me about how he was feeling at the time though because things could have worked out differently if he had.' She swapped the phone over to her other side, cradling it between her neck and shoulder before unscrewing the mascara and pulling out the wand.

There was a click, followed by heavy breathing. 'See I told you she was wavering where feck face was concerned, Rosie. I could see it in her face at lunch yesterday and honestly you want to have heard her going on this morning. She's over the hill, blah blah, and Marcus could be the 'one' blah blah, and what if she misses her chance? You'd think her ovaries were shrinking as we speak. She needs to toughen up and be like your woman what's her name? The one battling the big monster alien in that film.'

'Sigourney Weaver.'

'Yeah, her. She wouldn't take Marcus fecking coward McDonagh back, ovaries or no ovaries.'

'Moira get off the phone,' Aisling said. 'Now!'

She waited until she heard the click. 'She's going to be the end of me, so she is.'

'She's right, Ash, not about Sigourney Weaver—you're way too short to be like her. You do need to toughen up though and sure, you've loads of time to be worrying about your eggs and what not. Us O'Mara's we're from good childbearing stock. Look at Mam, she was nearly forty when Moira came along. Noah, put that back! He's only after helping himself to the chocolate biscuits because I'm on the phone and his dad's out for a run. And you know what she'd have to say on the subject.'

'Who?' Aisling was struggling to keep up with the conversation. She peered into the mirror and ran the wand under her lashes.

'Mammy, of course.'

Ah, God, here we go again, Aisling thought blinking and cursing to herself as a flurry of black dots appeared beneath her eye. 'What?'

'Marry in haste repent at leisure.'

'Ow!'

'What happened?'

'I stabbed myself in the eye with my mascara. I look like I'm heading off to an audition for KISS. Damn it.'

'You don't learn the fine art of multitasking until you've had a baby, Ash. And I'm done. I've said all I'm going to say to you on the subject of Marcus McDonagh.'

And pigs might fly, Aisling thought blinking furiously.

'Listen, if I don't put Noah on to say hello, he'll burst a blood vessel.'

Aisling grinned, 'Well we don't want that, stick him on.'

# Chapter 29

Aisling made it down the stairs with fifteen minutes to spare before she was due to meet Una. The weather looked fierce outside and she'd decided to wrap up warmly. It had been hard going, but she'd managed to squeeze into her black jeans, throw on a sweater and wrap a scarf around her neck. Lastly, she'd pulled her black boots with the silver buckling detail on over her jeans. She'd fallen in love with them after spotting them in the window of Debenhams in last year's sale. A quick check in the mirror that all those pesky mascara dots were gone, and she was good to go.

It was a relief to escape the apartment and her sister after the morning's debacle. Moira didn't look as though she intended rushing off anywhere; she was still in her pyjamas and in her happy place watching the EastEnders weekend omnibus. She'd barely looked up from the screen when Aisling said she'd catch her later.

'Morning, James, everything under control?' she said, descending the stairs to reception.

'Hi.' He swivelled around in his seat looking fresh faced, his dark hair artfully styled. Aisling wondered if he'd even started shaving yet. 'Grand, Aisling. It's been quiet, so far.' He looked at her for a beat but was too polite to ask why she was late down. It was after all completely out of character for her. 'Nobody's checked out yet, though Room 3 is due soon.'

'Yes, the Petersons are on the move today and the Prestons are leaving too.' She wondered idly whether the company had sold the young couple on relocating.

James brought up the screen on the computer and nodded, 'Mr Walsh's checking out too.'

Of course he was! Aisling had nearly forgotten he was going back to Liverpool today. It would have been dreadful if she hadn't said goodbye to him in person. It wasn't like her not to know the comings and goings of O'Mara's guests off the bat and especially a regular like Mr Walsh. It was this business with Marcus. He wasn't good for business!

'He'll be down having his breakfast. I'll go and say cheerio to him now. I'll take that downstairs, shall I?' She picked up the plate beside the computer. There was nothing left on it save a piece of bacon rind. Mr Fox would enjoy that later she thought.

The phone began to ring and James grinned giving her a thumbs up. 'Cheers, Aisling. Tell Mrs Baicu it hit the spot.'

Aisling smiled back. His mam probably sorted his breakfast at home before he left to come here, and then he no sooner he sat down to do some work and Mrs Baicu served him up a second great helping. Ah well, look at the Australian brothers staying with them at the moment, the Freeman boys. Mrs Flaherty had been in seventh heaven seeing their heaped plates hoovered up each morning.

Branok and Emblyn Nancarrow were making their way gingerly down the stairs. Aisling paused at the foot of them as they reached the landing above her and called out a good morning. They both looked rather crumpled and still half asleep. Relics from a bygone era in their flowing tie-dyed ensembles. She hoped they had layers on under all that garb or they'd freeze today.

'Thank you for your recommendation of Quinn's, Aisling. We had the most divine Irish stew followed by a slice of gateau, but I don't feel guilty,' Branok patted his middle, hidden beneath his loose shirt, 'because we worked it off after dinner by putting our dancing shoes on. The chap playing the fiddle had everybody up.'

'Branok forgets he's not in his twenties anymore and he was throwing himself about the floor like he was at Glastonbury or Woodstock. His body brings him up with a short shrift reminder the next day though,' Emblyn said. 'We're both in need of a good strong cup of coffee I'm afraid.' She yawned to demonstrate her point.

Aisling laughed, 'Well, you'll find a pot brewed downstairs. Mrs Baicu hails from Romania and her coffee is thick and strong. A bit like Turkish coffee.'

'Just what we need, Emblyn.' She nodded her agreement.

'A cup of that and a plate piled high with bacon and eggs will see you both right.' Aisling flashed them a smile before glancing at Una's door on her way past Room 1. Perhaps she should knock in case she'd slept in. She hesitated but then decided to leave it and carried on down the stairs. She was more than likely getting dressed, or she may even be downstairs having breakfast. Either way, if she wasn't in the guest lounge at eleven, she'd tap on her door.

The dining room was busy, and Aisling smiled and greeted the guests, pausing to check in with Mrs Baicu who had Geraldine beavering away buttering toast. They were a well-oiled machine, and she'd only get underfoot were she to linger in the kitchen so she made a beeline for Mr Walsh.

He was ever the gentlemen, dapper in his suit. There was no such word as casual in his world and getting up he pulled the seat out for her.

'That colour's becoming on you, Aisling.'

She glanced at the maroon scarf draped over her sweater. 'Thank you. It's a sad day to be sure, Mr Walsh, what with you leaving us again to cross the water,' Aisling twinkled. She sat down opposite him shaking her head and putting her hand over the cup to signal that she was alright when he gestured to the teapot. 'The weather certainly thinks so, it's tipping down outside.'

'Ah, Aisling, as much as it pains my heart, I have to leave. I'm a man with commitments. I've a dog needs picking up from the kennels and a garden that will be due some attention,' he bantered back.

'We'll miss you.'

It was true. Aisling had a lot of time for Mr Walsh. She could tell he had a kind heart. She wondered about his life in Liverpool. She had a vague idea he'd been a salesman or something like before he'd retired. He certainly had the necessary charm for that line of work. Her eyes strayed to his left hand and she wondered if he had a lady friend. There was no ring on his finger to signal he'd ever been married and was perhaps widowed. Then again, he could be divorced, the ring tucked away in a drawer forgotten about. It was none of her business either way.

'Be sure to tell Bronagh I said goodbye now won't you. She's a good woman that one.'

Aisling might not have had much in the way of sleep the night before and her brain may have only been running at half capacity but there was something in his tone of voice. It was the way his expression seemed to lighten and lift when Bronagh's name rolled off his tongue. It had her matchmaking antennae all a quiver. She did the maths. Bronagh had never married, she lived with her ailing mammy. Mr Walsh would appear to be something of a bachelor. If she were a few years older, quite a few years older she'd have him pegged as a catch. One plus one equalled three! It was a match Moira would wholeheartedly approve of.

'I'll pass it on to her, Mr Walsh. You know we're only a phone call away. Keep in touch, won't you? Don't leave it a whole year until we hear from you again.' She wanted to add that Bronagh's hours were eight am until four pm Monday to Friday, she was single so far as Aisling knew, and if he wished to correspond with her, Aisling would happily forward all mail on. She thought that might be a little obvious however and refrained. She caught sight of his watch face, the time had ticked over to eleven o'clock. She couldn't sit here any longer pondering subtle ways in which to orchestrate further contact between this dapper gent and her receptionist but as she made to get up from her seat, she had a brainwave.

'Mr Walsh, I've got to dash, I'm due to meet a friend but, you know, I just realised you're not on our Christmas card list. That's a sin, so it is, what with you being our favourite guest and all. Why don't you leave your address with James at the front desk?'

Mr Walsh nodded and at that moment Mrs Baicu, her dark hair silvered with grey scraped back in a bun, burst through the kitchen doors and marched toward them. An efficient, angular woman who always reminded Aisling of a Liquorice Allsort, she put this down to her multi-coloured voluminous peasant skirts. She wore the same style of skirt no matter what the season and, if it was cold she pulled on woollen tights. Today was definitely a woollen tights day. Her accent still echoed strongly of her Eastern European roots. 'Mr Walsh you can't leave without this.' She thrust a glass jar at him, its contents a dark and syrupy jam secured by a twist-top lid. 'It's what we Romanian's call magiun, plum jam. A speciality of mine. It would give me great pleasure to know you were enjoying this on your toast each morning once you are back in Liverpool. You spread the word the Romanian jam is good, yes?'

Aisling's mouth twitched. It was a good job Mrs Flaherty wasn't here. The two cooks were fiercely competitive over their jam making skills. If she were to get wind Mrs Baicu was giving their regulars samples of her traditional plum jam to take home, there'd be a good deal of fecking. It would be followed by a shortage of oranges in Dublin as she set about whipping up her marmalade for all and sundry staying at O'Mara's.

Aisling wished Mr Walsh all the best for his journey home and leaving Mrs Baicu fussing over him she made her way up the stairs and through to the guest lounge.

Una was perched on the same chair she'd been sitting in only a few hours earlier. The green quilted dressing gown, however, had been replaced. She was wearing the same cardigan and skirt combo as yesterday along with the blue blouse Aisling had complimented her on. Somehow, she looked less severe this morning. It was down to the splash of subtle colour from the lipstick and blush she'd applied, Aisling realised. For a woman who'd been up half the night, she looked surprisingly well although her anxiety was palpable. Her hands were clasped so tightly in her lap her knuckles were white. Aisling tried to put her at ease.

'Did you manage to get a little more sleep, Una? You certainly look rested.'

'I did, thank you, I went out like a light. I'd still be asleep now if I hadn't set the alarm. Yourself?'

'Me too. Have you had time for breakfast?' It dawned on her she'd been too busy battling Roisin and Moira off earlier to grab anything. She could have helped herself to what was on offer in Mrs Baicu's kitchen, but she'd gotten caught up chatting to Mr Walsh. Ah well, it wouldn't do her any harm and her stomach was beginning churn on Una's behalf, anyway.

'No, I couldn't, dear, not this morning.'

They were a right pair. Aisling gave her a smile to say she understood. 'I'll get James to call us a taxi, shall I? Oh, and if you've a coat with you it might be an idea to put it on. It's a miserable old Sunday out there.'

Una nodded, 'I'll go and get it now, shall I?'

'Grand.'

# Chapter 30

A isling was sitting in the back of the taxi, Una in the front. She glanced at her profile. The hood of her rain jacket was bunched around her shoulders. Her gaze was fixed straight ahead, and her mouth set in a firm line. She looked away to stare out the window, rivulets of water were running down. It was bucketing down; they were getting a taste of the winter to come today for sure.

Their driver, she'd seen when he strode cheerily into O'Mara's announcing his arrival, had a bulbous red nose. He also had the telltale broken capillaries of a man who was partial to a glass or two—they formed a network to rival the London Underground across both his cheeks.

Now he began intrepidly trying to engage his two passengers in cheerful patter about the gloomy day and where they might be off to on a wet Sunday morning. Neither Una nor Aisling replied with more than the bare minimum of conversation necessary so as not to appear rude. They were both worn out from the talking they'd done through the night and were content to sit in silence, lost in their own thoughts.

The driver heaved a sigh and gave up as he drove them over the Liffey. All they could hear as they reached the red brick suburb in which Aideen lived was the ticking over of the meter, the sluicing tyres as they rolled through the puddles, and an annoying jaw-clicking sound the driver was making. It was painful to listen to.

187

'It's just up there, if you pull over beside the park that will do nicely, thank you.' Una gestured to the wedge of dull green grass up ahead on the left.

'Are you sure? You'll get soaked so you will. Can I drop you to the door of wherever it is you're going?'

'Thank you, no. We'll be fine.' Una was curt, her voice tense. 'What do I owe you?'

Aisling opened her purse, but Una was insistent she pay as the driver idled the car. There was no point arguing and, getting out of the car, she popped her umbrella. The street was quiet with a row of cars parked along one side nose to nose. There were no signs of human life, but she wasn't surprised; they weren't a country of early risers. Her eyes flitted over the deserted park. The play area stood in the middle, empty and forlorn. She saw a tree, its branches drooping under the rain, a bench seat beneath it, and surmised that was where Una had been whiling away her days since she'd been in Dublin. The sight of it saddened her.

Aideen's house was one of the houses in the row of smart terraces across the road. How would they be received? Aisling hoped the sight of her sister standing on her doorstep after all these years didn't prove too much of a shock for Aideen. She wasn't well after all. Aisling was nearly as anxious as Una who appeared beside her a beat later. Her face was pale and apprehensive as she peered out from under her rain jacket's hood. Aisling held her umbrella up over both of them while they waited for the taxi to drive away. Then she linked her arm through Una's—to offer reassurance and to make sure she didn't try to change her mind as they crossed the road.

The house Una halted outside was opposite the park.

'This is Aideen's, number eighteen.'

Aisling opened the gate and keeping a firm grip on Una walked up the front path. Despite the time of year, the garden was neatly kept, the foliage trimmed back for winter, and the path led them to a cheery red door. It had the shiniest brass knocker she'd ever seen. Aideen was obviously house proud and before Una could protest, Aisling lifted it and rapped three times. Aisling could feel Una's body ramrod and rigid next to her as they waited. The seconds stretched long.

'She's not home, we'll come another time.'

'Una, she'll have barely had time to get out of her chair. Give it a minute.'

Aisling crossed her fingers that Aideen was home. She didn't fancy her chances of getting Una back here again. Her gut told her if the sisters didn't reconnect today it wouldn't happen. Una would get back on the train and chug away for good.

They should have gotten the driver to wait even if that jaw clicking thing was annoying. It was not the day to be standing on the side of the road waiting for taxis. She picked up the knocker and rapped it twice more, willing Aideen to open the door. She'd count to twenty really slowly and if no one had answered by then they'd have to go. They couldn't loiter on her front doorstep all day, the neighbours would get suspicious and they'd wind up with pneumonia.

'I really think we should leave.' Una shifted impatiently.

Aisling had counted to fifteen. She sighed, maybe Una was right. Hang on, she could hear movement. She squeezed Una's arm in nervous anticipation.

'Someone's coming.'

She heard the sharp intake of breath next to her as the door opened.

# Chapter 31

The sisters stared in open mouthed silence at each other, and Aisling stared from one to the other. She knew, of course, that Una and Aideen were twins but the reality of seeing Una's double standing in the entrance of her home was still a shock. They were identical twins but the difference between them was glaringly obvious. Aideen's face had a puffiness to it and her eyes were hollow with dark shadows beneath them. Her head was covered by a scarf and Aisling noticed it was the exact cheerful shade of cornflower blue as Una's blouse. She was dressed in a pretty lilac jumper with grey trousers with fluffy pink slippers on her feet.

'Una,' Aideen whispered finally, clasping the door as though frightened she might fall. 'Is it really you?'

Una nodded and then launched herself on her sister who nearly did fall backwards as she was wrapped in a soggy embrace. Aisling could hear Una's sobs mingling with her muffled, 'I'm sorry, I left it too long, I'm so sorry.'

'So am I. Shush, it doesn't matter now. None of it matters anymore. You came. That's what counts.'

Aisling wasn't sure if it was droplets of rain or tears running down her face as she watched the sisters embrace. She suspected the latter. She couldn't imagine not having seen either of her sisters for so many years. Oh, they drove each other to distraction most of the time, but they were always there for each other when it mattered. Aideen looked over her shoulder at Aisling questioningly. It dawned on her that she might assume she was Una's daughter and she quickly jumped in before there could be any misunderstanding.

'I'm Aisling O'Mara. Una's staying at my family's guest-house, O'Mara's.'

'The guesthouse on the green?'

'Yes.'

'You always wanted to stay there, Una.'

Una broke away and turned toward Aisling. 'I did. Aisling and I haven't known each other long, but she's been a good friend to me, Aideen. I don't know if I'd have had the courage to come today if it wasn't for her.'

'When did you arrive in Dublin?'

'Midweek, I've come every day to see you. I've sat over there,' she gestured to the park, 'trying to pluck up the nerve to knock on your door but I couldn't. Not on my own.'

'I'd have never turned you away, Una. You must have known that.'

'I was frightened. Scared I'd left it too long to put things right.'

'Never. Una. My door's always been open for you.' Aideen registered that they were all standing in the doorway. 'Come inside both of you before you catch a chill. Una, we'll hang that wet coat up and I'll put the kettle on.'

'That sounds lovely, thank you,' Aisling said. She'd stay awhile to be polite, besides which a cuppa would go down a treat. She was freezing! She closed the umbrella leaving it to stand on the doorstep as she followed behind Una. Aideen closed the door and fussed around taking Una's coat and hanging it on a hook. Aisling took the opportunity to look around her. They were in the hallway, stairs leading off it to the upstairs where the bedrooms would be. There was a room off the hall on either side. A living room and a dining room no doubt. Aideen must have been in the kitchen Aisling surmised seeing the light was on at the end of the hall. It explained why it had taken her a while to answer the door.

Photographs lined the walls and a quick glance proved them to be family portraits. A montage of Aideen and Leo's boys over the years. How boisterous Aideen's life would have been bringing up her boys compared to her sister's. They were mischievous looking little lads who'd grown into handsome young men. There were grandchildren too she saw. Six of them if the photograph of them looking angelic in a formal garden setting was anything to go by.

Her eyes settled on a wedding photo, curious to see what Leo looked like. He was handsome in his suit and Aideen was a beautiful bride but she fancied she could see a sadness in her eyes lurking beneath the surface. Maybe she was being fanciful. As for Leo he was just a man, rather ordinary truth be told, but both sisters had seen so much more in him. Who would have thought his love could cause so much distress? The same could be said about Marcus she supposed.

'Do you remember Mam's friend, Maire Reynolds,' Una was saying.

'Of course. She liked her tea strong enough for a mouse to trot on!'

The sisters smiled at the mutual memory.

They had so much shared history and so much they didn't know about each other's lives, Aisling thought. It would be a day full of chatter as they desperately tried to catch up on their lost years. A light glowed invitingly in the kitchen and she followed Una and Aideen toward it.

'I keep the heating on high in here.' Aideen was saying.

The room was indeed toasty, and Aisling enjoyed the tingling warmth spreading through her cold limbs. It was a small kitchen in need of updating but functional, nevertheless. The window over the sink overlooked the garden where an empty washing line spun around in the wind.

I hope it's not too much of a sauna for you. But I feel the cold these days since I began the chemo.'

Una made an odd sound.

'It's alright, Una, everything's going to be alright now you'll see,' Aideen said going through the motions of making a pot of tea. 'Because you're here.'

# Chapter 32

Aisling drank her tea enjoying listening to the sisters animated conversation as they talked overtop of one another. Their eagerness to fill each other in on their lives meant the plate of digestive biscuits Aideen had set out along with the tea were ignored. Just one more Aisling told herself. She was partial to a tea biscuit and she gave it a brief dunk before chomping into it watching the sisters' shared gestures and mannerisms with fascination. They were mirror images, peas in a pod.

She let herself be transported along with them back to their childhood as they relived their younger days. She could see where those boys she'd peered up at in the photographs in the hallway got their mischievous streak from. She'd happily while away the rest of the afternoon in Aideen's snug kitchen drinking tea and polishing off the biscuits, listening to their tales, but that wouldn't be fair. She was a third wheel even if she had been made welcome. A yawn escaped unbidden and she was aware of being lulled by the warmth and the lilt of their voices. It was time she made tracks and stopped earwigging.

'Aideen, Una, I'm sorry to interrupt but I should really be getting back to O'Mara's.'

They looked at her startled, pulled from their reminiscing. It was as though they'd forgotten she was even in the room with them. They probably had she realised, asking Aideen if she'd mind if she borrowed her phone to call a taxi.

'Of course not, dear. It's on the table in the hallway help yourself.'

Aisling rang the number she knew by heart having called it a thousand times before for guests. She spieled off the address and was told the taxi wouldn't be long. She glanced up again at the wedding photo that had caught her eye earlier as she hung up the phone. It was nice to think Leo was looking down on Aideen and Una, a silent witness from up there in heaven to their reunion. He'd be happy she thought, studying his face. It was kind, and she knew he'd have had no wish to cause the rift he had by misplacing his affections on Una. She could see the devotion on Aideen's face as she smiled up at him frozen in time, but yes there was a definite sadness there too. What a choice they'd had to make, and their happiness had come at a high price.

She hoped, as she made her way back to the kitchen to say her goodbyes, that Aideen and Una had plenty of time left together. That this chapter of their lives would be happy. Perhaps Una would prove to be the tonic Aideen needed to overcome her illness.

Aideen was telling Una of all the different ways in which she'd learned to tie her headscarf since her hair had begun to fall out as she entered the room and Aisling inadvertently raised her hand to her own hair; despite the umbrella it had gotten wet and had dried in ratty spirals.

'My taxi won't be long so I'll say cheerio to you both now and thank you for your hospitality, Aideen.' She was on the receiving end of warm hugs when a horn sounded from the street outside. She would see Una again and hear what her plans were from this point forward. Who knew, she might even see

Aideen again—she hoped so. She wished her all the very best and left her to catch up with her sister. She was looking forward to doing some catching up of her own tonight with Leila and Quinn. It had been ages since she'd had a good laugh with her old pals and she was well overdue to catch up on all their news.

The driver having tooted his arrival was a clue, Aisling thought five minutes into the journey home, as to his sullen un-communicative manner. She stole a sideways glance at him. His surly expression said he was clearly not living his dream. Bring back the jaw clicker! She focussed her attention on the road ahead, not really seeing it though as she pondered Marcus. Her head was spinning with all that had happened in the last forty-eight hours. She wouldn't call him today. She wasn't ready. Seeing Leila would give her another perspective and she'd hash it over with her tonight. Leila dealt with the business of love on a daily basis so hopefully she could offer some advice that would help her decide whether giving him another chance might lead to her happy ending. One thing she knew for certain was she couldn't cope with having her trust shattered a second time.

Quinn's face floated before her. He had such an infectious grin. An old memory fought its way through. They'd gone ten-pin bowling and he'd let her win. As the victor, it had been her responsibility to buy chips on the way home. A grand debate had been waged in the chipper over drowning them in curry sauce or eating them plain with salt and vinegar. Aisling was partial to the curry sauce, Quinn said it was sacrilege. They'd had such a laugh that night. She quashed the familiar pang but not before remembering how he'd let her have her way with the curry sauce.

The taxi pulled up across the road from O'Mara's and Aisling paid him. She wasn't a tipper but even if she was that way inclined, he didn't deserve one. As if he'd read her mind, he sped off, spraying her with water much to her chagrin, though she managed to refrain from giving him a rude finger sign. She waited impatiently for a break in the traffic and ran across the road, keen to get out of the weather. Evie was on the desk and looked up startled when she barrelled in through the door shaking herself off like a dog.

'You look like a drowned rat.'

'Cheers.'

'Have you been out with yer man, Marcus, then?'

Straight to the point. She really was a nosy madam. Aisling toyed with the idea of telling her that she'd had a delightful morning riding her ex and the cobwebs had well and truly been blown away. It would almost be worth it to see the shock on her smug little face. It was on the tip of her tongue, but she held back. A lie like that however satisfying would be cutting her nose off to spite her face and God help her if it got back to Mammy!

'I've been out with one of our guests, actually.' And that was as much information as she was going to give her. 'Right, I'd best get into some dry gear.'

She left Evie pondering who the guest might be and why Aisling had ventured out on such a miserable day with them. That morsel of information would keep her amused all afternoon as she tried to solve the mystery—a regular little Nancy Drew.

Moira was sitting where she'd left her, still glued to the television although her favourite show would have finished by now. She called out a cursory greeting. This time her sister switched the set off and focussed her attention on her. 'Where've you been? Mammy called. Her sailing lesson got cancelled and she wanted to chat. I told her I couldn't cos EastEnders was on but seeing how it was an ad break I'd go downstairs and nab you instead. I didn't know you were heading out.' Her tone was accusatory.

It was like she was a wayward teen and Moira was the mam desperately trying to keep her in line. 'You wouldn't have heard me if I'd told you where I was going, anyway. You were too involved in whatever was happening in Albert Square this week.' The soap opera was almost a religious experience for Moira and you did not interrupt her when she was watching it. 'Give me ten minutes to have a shower, I need to warm up, then I'll tell you what I've been up to. Oh and by the way it doesn't involve Marcus if that's what you were thinking.'

Aisling clambered out of her wet gear and put her dressing gown on. She carried the damp clothes through to the kitchen and left them to whir around in the dryer before sitting down next to Moira. As there were two mugs of tea on the coffee table, she decided the hot shower could wait a little longer, and then she could think about getting ready for her date with Leila and Quinn.

'I made you one.' Moira stated.

'Thanks.' Aisling picked hers up. It was out of character for her sister to get off her arse and make her a cuppa, but she wouldn't look a gift horse in the mouth. She realised what had just run through her mind and shuddered. She really was morphing into Mammy with all her little sayings—a gift horse in the mouth, what did that even mean for goodness sake? She had a sip and felt the sweet hot liquid warm her right through. 'Oh, that's good.'

Moira looked pleased with herself. 'So come on then, where've you been.'

'Well, you know the guest in Room 1, Una Brennan?'

'The battleaxe who's got a face on her like someone farted. You should have seen her giving me the hairy eyeball the other morning when I was under the weather.'

'Jeez, Moira, you come out with it. Yes, her, only she's not such a battleaxe, listen to this.' Aisling didn't think Una would mind her sharing her story with Moira, not with how things had worked out today. She filled her in on the Brennan twins' story and Moira listened wide-eyed. She wasn't as hard as she liked to make out. Aisling saw her eyes well up when she got to the part where Una hadn't long been out of the hospital and Leo had told her he'd realised it was Aideen he loved.

By the time she'd finished her tale, Moira was reaching for the tissues. 'Jaysus, that was worse than when Tiffany Mitchell got run over by Frank Butcher.'

Aisling assumed she was referring to an EastEnders plot but didn't dwell on it further because the phone began to ring. It was probably Mammy ringing back. A beat later hearing the familiar voice she knew she'd guessed correctly.

'Aisling, is that you?'

Mammy always sounded surprised when she answered the phone. It probably stemmed from all those years working abroad. You'd think she'd have gotten used to her being home by now though. 'Yes, it's me. How're ya keepin', Mammy?'

'Ah grand, although I'm at a bit of a loose end. My sailing got cancelled and I can't very well go and play golf in this weather unless I want to put my bathers on and have a round with the ducks.' She sighed as though the weight of the world rested on her shoulders.

Maureen O'Mara was a people person. She didn't like rattling about on her own and was in her element when her social calendar was full. The idea of a day at home by herself followed by more of the same in the evening would fill her with fear. Mother and middle child were different like that. Aisling enjoyed her own company and hated having a social calendar that was full to the brim—not that there was much chance of that these days. Musings aside she got what her mammy was hinting at. 'Did you want to come over this evening for some company?'

'For dinner? Now that would be lovely, I'll be there by seven at the latest.' The phone went dead before Aisling could say that she wouldn't be home. Of course, Mammy would assume she'd be home for the night given she hadn't been out for the evening in an absolute age. She got a glint in her eyes. It was payback time for Moira's behaviour this morning.

Moira, what're your plans tonight?'

She looked a little glum. 'I was hoping to hear from a friend.' She picked up her phone and eyed the screen before dropping it by her side. 'But I haven't and it's not likely I will now.'

'What friend?'

'Oh, no one you know, just someone from work.' This was said quickly and Aisling glanced at her sister sharply. She caught a glimpse of that secretive closed Mona Lisa face once more but Moira moved on before she could delve into what she was up to.

'How's about going halvesies on a takeaway?' said Moira 'I'm starved with the hunger. How's about lemon chicken and maybe a black bean beef with fried rice.'

There it was again, the assumption she'd be sitting in. It annoyed Aisling. 'Actually, I'm out tonight, NOT with Marcus!' she shot back at her sister before she could open her mouth. 'I'm meeting Leila at Quinn's for your information. Mammy's on her way round though, she'll go you halvesies. She's partial to black bean beef. I'd get out of those pyjamas though if I were you or you'll never hear the end of it.'

Aisling left Moira muttering under her breath and headed off to get ready. She planned to make her escape before Mammy arrived. The only person she wanted to talk to about Marcus tonight was Leila.

# Chapter 33

It was a little ridiculous calling a taxi to travel the short distance from O'Mara's to Quinn's, but there was no way Aisling was going to arrive at the restaurant soaked and looking like a bedraggled sea creature washed ashore. Not when she'd spent an age dolling herself up. Nor would she risk her Jimmy Choo glitter mules—a bargain so far as Jimmy Choo's went—bought in the sales several years ago, encountering a puddle. Truth be told and puddles aside she wasn't sure she could walk more than a block in the heels. They defied gravity even by her standards.

She'd made a special effort tonight and she wasn't sure why. Leila and Quinn wouldn't care if she turned up in her pyjamas. Speaking of which Moira had finally gotten dressed. The thought of the lecture she'd be sure to receive from Mammy on falling into slovenly ways was all the incentive needed.

Aisling had faffed with her make-up and hair before sliding into her little black dress—actually she'd wriggled her way into it. She hadn't been sure if it would fit, but she managed to wrestle the zipper into place, completing her outfit with the crème de la crème pair of shoes in her collection. It was as though she were putting on armour she'd mused, giving herself a final once over. Proving to herself that she was in control of what happened next in her life. She sucked her tummy in and smoothed the dress down; she didn't scrub up too badly. It was nice to get dressed up. She used to all the time. She'd forgotten what a boost it always gave her.

'Give Mammy a hug from me,' she said before singing out a cheery 'Bye' to Moira. She had a face on her. A night in watching Ballykissangel with Mammy could do that to a girl. It was her habit of talking to the characters throughout the show telling them what they should be doing. Ah well, Moira would cheer up once she had a helping of lemon chicken in front of her. Aisling pondered on what she'd order tonight remembering the Irish Baileys cheesecake she'd spied on the menu board. Her tummy rumbled reminding her all she'd had to eat today was tea biscuits.

Aisling gripped the banister tightly as she gingerly descended the stairs, it had been a long time since the Jimmy Choo's had had an outing. She was out of practice but sure wearing high heels was second nature to her. Give her an hour and she'd be up for a marathon. She tottered through into reception, head held high. It was deserted apart from Evie who was eating a bowl of two-minute noodles with an unenthusiastic expression. Her face lit up when she spied her boss though. 'Wow, Aisling you look gorgeous—like a film star. I love those shoes.'

Aisling felt herself soften toward the younger girl. Give her a compliment and she was anybody's. 'Thanks, Evie.'

'You must be going somewhere special?'

Fishing, always fishing. 'For dinner with friends. Oh, there's my taxi. Have a good night.'

'Mind how you go.'

Aisling swept out into the night. Things were off to a good start she thought, seeing the driver had the good manners to get out of the taxi to hold the door open for her. That surly fecker from earlier could learn a few tricks from him she thought sliding onto the backseat. Her hand reached up and patted her hair; it was still intact. Yes, a good start to the evening indeed.

Quinn's was heaving. She'd forgotten what a big night Sundays were. Alasdair didn't disappoint. He gave her a once over that from anybody else would be offensive followed by a long slow whistle. 'Aisling O'Mara, I swear you're fit for the red carpet. Tonight you have me in mind of Ginger Rogers when we featured in Swing Time together.'

Before Aisling knew what was happening Alasdair was doing his best Fred Astaire tap-dancing impersonation and had grabbed hold of her, giving her a twirl. It was a dance move that would have ended in disaster had he not had a firm hold of her. 'Love those shoes by the way. Divine!' He let her go. She was aware of other patrons looking on in amusement and a few were clapping, but she was far too used to Alasdair's flamboyant ways to be embarrassed.

Quinn was standing in the doorway of the kitchen giving her a slow clap along with a big grin. She could see he'd shaved even from where she was standing. She gave him a little bow before scanning the tables to see if Leila, ever punctual, had beaten her there. She had and was laughing at the display she'd just witnessed. She waved.

Aisling left Alasdair to accost the patrons who'd ducked in from the rain. They were making a show of rubbing their hands and stamping their feet as though they'd just escaped from a howling blizzard. She weaved her way around to the table in the far corner of the room. Alasdair had arranged for them to be as far away from the stage as possible, so they could hear themselves speak. A solitary amp and microphone were the only clues there'd be live music later. Aisling hoped Quinn planned on joining them too and wasn't going to spend the evening slaving in the kitchen.

Leila stood up to greet her friend with a warm hug. She smelt gorgeous Aisling thought, inhaling an unfamiliar scent. Leila looked down at Aisling's feet.

'Ooh, the Jimmy Choo's, my favourite. You look gorgeous, Ash. I love that dress.'

'Thank you, I wasn't sure if it would still fit but I managed to squeeze into it. I'll be fine so long as I don't eat!' she laughed. 'You do too but then you always do.' Leila with her petite figure and lustrous blonde hair didn't have to make much effort. She could wear a sack and look stylish. Tonight she'd opted for a simple pale blue shift dress with bell sleeves. Her hair was loose, framing her pretty pixie face. 'And you smell divine, what is that?'

'I treated myself, it's a new Gucci fragrance called Rush.'

'It suits you.'

They sat down and both began to talk at once, laughing at their eagerness to catch up. Aisling giggled as Leila relayed a tale about a recent wedding where the bride had gotten tipsy and called her new mother-in-law an old trout. They'd no time to move on to other topics before a waiter Aisling hadn't seen before made a beeline for their table. He looked like a student, whose mam had told him to put on his good shirt, trying to earn a bit of cash on the side.

'Hello, there. I'm Tom your waiter this evening. Now then can I get you both something to drink before you check out our menu?'

'Hi, Tom. Yes, please. Leila, should we share a bottle of red?'

'Why not.'

'A bottle of your house red please, Tom. Oh, and would you mind telling Quinn to get his arse out here and come and join us?'

Tom grinned and put his pencil behind his ear, 'I will. Shall I use those words exactly?'

'Definitely.'

He moved away to pass on the message.

'So, moving right along. Dare I ask have you seen Marcus since I spoke to you?'

'I have, he was waiting for me when I got home from lunch with Moira and Mammy on Saturday afternoon.'

'And?'

'You can probably guess what he had to say for himself.'

Leila nodded. 'How did you leave things or am I better off not knowing?'

'I promised him I'd think about what he'd said. He's staying with his mam and dad. As for any of that other stuff it's been so long, I've forgotten how.'

'Sure it's like riding a bike. Not that I'm encouraging you to get back on that particular bicycle.'

Aisling raised an eyebrow, glad to divert the conversation away from Marcus. She only went around in circles where he was concerned. 'That sounds like someone who's been doing a spot of pedalling recently.'

Leila smiled. 'I might have gone for a tandem ride after the third date with a photographer fella I met at a wedding. I have my standards you know.'

'Glad to hear it, and what is this photographer fella's name then?'

Leila mumbled something and Aisling strained to hear it but couldn't catch it.

'What was that?'

Leila sighed. 'Don't you dare laugh.'

'I won't.'

'Bearach, it means Barry.'

Aisling snorted before erupting into peals of laughter. 'Sorry, Leila, but Bearach?' She tried it out for size, 'Ooh, Bearach. Or, ooh, Barry! I don't know what's worse,' she choked.

'I knew you'd take the mickey.' Leila grinned. 'And for the record, I am not a moaner.'

Tom arrived with their glasses and a bottle of red which, for someone of his tender years, he opened with a flourish before leaving it to breathe.

'Bugger all that breathing business I need a drink after that.' Aisling poured them both a glass and raised hers. 'A toast. May you have warm words on a cold evening, a full moon on dark nights, and the road downhill all the way to your door.' They clinked glasses.

'Where did you get that from?'

'One of our guest's souvenir tea towels. I liked it.'

Quinn, having checked all was ticking over in his kitchen made his way over. 'Hello, my two favourite ladies, may I join you?'

'Of course, sit your arse down.'

He grinned and did as he was told. Aisling, spying Tom about to move away from a nearby table, called out, 'Tom, would you mind getting us another glass please?' She had to smile watching the young waiter, seeing it was his boss who required the vessel, virtually run to the bar. He returned a beat later making a show of polishing the glass before pouring a generous amount of the ruby liquid into it. He stood back cloth draped over his arm waiting for approval. It was too late for Quinn to do a tasting, given Aisling had already drunk half the contents of her glass. Leila had had a good go at hers too. Nevertheless, Quinn played the game. He held the glass up to the light and swirled it before sniffing the contents and finally taking a sip.

Aisling's heart skipped a beat as a memory of Marcus came to the fore. She knew wine connoisseurs did this to get a sense of the wine—at least this what Marcus had told her. He was a spitter, and insisted on performing the ritual whenever they ate out. She hated it, finding it a seat-squirming, pretentious show—especially if he waved it away for whatever reason. It had taken the enjoyment out of the evening for her on more than one occasion. Funny she mused, she'd forgotten that. Not to mention it was a waste of good wine!

Quinn swallowed, and Aisling exhaled.

'Cheers, Tom. That hit the spot. Bottoms up ladies.' He raised his glass and clinked with Leila and Aisling. Tom asked if they were ready to order.

Quinn picked the menus up off the table and passed them up to Tom. 'There's no need for these. These two are old friends of mine and I've prepared something special for them.'

Aisling and Leila clapped their hands in delight—they were in for a treat.

'I hope you're hungry.'

'I could eat the back door buttered,' Aisling grinned.

# Chapter 34

True to his word Quinn had indeed produced something special. He disappeared into the kitchen returning a few moments later with an enormous platter which he set down in the centre of the table. Tom materialised with a side plate for each of them before flapping napkins open to spread onto their laps. Aisling's mouth watered as she gazed down at the array of nibbles Quinn had created. It must have taken him hours to put together.

'This looks amazing thank you! How spoilt are we?'

Leila uttered the same sentiment.

'Ah well, you know me. I never miss a chance to show off in the kitchen. It's just a little something I threw together.' It was tongue in cheek. Aisling knew how to throw something together. It usually involved retrieving whatever was left over from last night's dinner from the refrigerator and reheating it. This, sitting on the table ready for them to tuck into, was art on a plate.

'Of course, if we were doing the proper degustation dining experience then I'd be bringing these out for you to sample plate by plate and pairing each dish with a complementing wine. I wanted to join you though not keep running off to the kitchen, besides I figured I'd be wasting my time walking you two lushes through the different wines.'

Leila waved the near empty bottle, 'Ah, the cheek. But you figured right. Another bottle of the house red will do us nicely, thank you very much.' She caught Tom's eye and he gave her the thumbs up. 'I'm almost frightened to eat anything it looks so pretty,' Leila said her attention returning to the platter of food in front of them.

'Well now that would be a waste. Here why don't you begin with this,' Quinn used the tongs and placed one of the dainty colourful morsels he'd selected on a side plate for each of them. 'My personal favourite. Seared scallop drizzled with pea puree on a cauliflower rösti.' He popped his in his mouth. 'That's good,' he mumbled through his mouthful, 'if I do say so myself. Come on you two. It's not like you to hold back.'

'Don't mind if I do,' Aisling grinned before demolishing hers, Leila following suit. Aisling had worked her way around to a generous sliver of smoky maple pork belly by the time Quinn, in between bites and wiping his mouth with a napkin, had finished regaling them with a kitchen disaster story involving an exploding pressure cooker. She made a mental note to never dig out Mammy's old one. It could stay tucked away down the back of the cupboard.

As they began to make short work of the food, they laughed over their student days and the things they used to get up to. Aisling leaned back in her chair, taking a breather from stuffing her face. She was feeling relaxed and merry. It was a tonic sharing wine and good food with her two most favourite people in the world, family aside.

Quinn, she thought, feeling a warm glow as she looked at him across the table had been such a good friend to her, especially during those awful weeks before Dad had passed. Leila too had stepped up above and beyond the call of duty, both when Dad died and after Marcus left. She resolved there and then to get the three of them together more regularly from thereon in. 'So,' she twinkled over her glass, not wanting to get too sentimental. 'I've heard about Leila's latest fling with Bearach, otherwise known as, *Ooh Barry*.' It earned her a kick under the table.

Quinn took Aisling's cue and began to chant, 'Leila and Bazzer up a tree—' he got no further before Leila threatened him with a Cajun spiced chicken wing and he held his hands up in surrender.

'You two are worse than children!'

They grinned across the table conspiratorially and Aisling hoped her teeth weren't black from the wine. She picked up with what she'd been about to say. 'Like I said, Quinn, we know who's been parking his boots under Leila's bed, but what about you?'

'Did you just blush?' Leila squealed, eager for payback.

'I did not. I've nothing to blush over. You know me, married to my business.'

'Ah, but your business won't keep you warm at night.' Leila demolished her chicken wing and wiping her greasy fingers on a napkin said, 'There must be a lovely foodie lass out there for you. A girl who knows her rump from her sirloin. It's a waste a fine-looking chap like yourself being on his own. I think what you need to do is come along to one of my weddings. They're chock full of young ladies all desperate to find Mr Right. We'll smuggle you in under the pretence of, oh I don't know being my assistant. We could call you Fabio or something like that,' she sniggered. 'What do you say?'

Aisling's insides twisted. How would she feel when Quinn met someone he was serious about? She didn't want to think about it.

'No fecking way,' he said.

Leila pouted. 'I think it's a great idea and I seem to recall you saying exactly that to me once before.'

'When?'

'When I suggested we all give salsa a go.'

'I wasn't keen initially either. You were good at it though, Quinn, a natural,' Aisling said. 'You should have stuck with it.'

'So were you.' Their eyes met both knowing why she hadn't continued. Salsa hadn't been Marcus's thing. It hadn't been Leila's either, but she'd have kept going for both their sakes. Quinn had called it quits when Aisling said she wouldn't be going back. The shine had gone out of it for him.

'What about you then, Aisling?' Quinn asked.

She shrugged and drained the dregs from her glass. 'What about me?'

'Any budding romances we should know about?' He reached over and filled her glass in an effort to busy himself.

'Marcus is back in town, and he wants her back.'

Quinn sloshed the wine over the side of Aisling's glass. 'Shit, sorry.'

'It's only a splash,' Aisling said, dabbing at the pink stain.

'What are you going to do?' Quinn sat back in his chair finishing the rest of his drink too quickly.

'I don't know. I've had an earful from Mammy, Roisin, and Moira as to what I should do—all of it involving telling him to feck off. Oh, and I believe calling him a ballbag was mentioned

more than once too. Come on, you two know me better than
anyone else, what do you think I should do?'

'Ash, we can't tell you what you should do, you know that.
You have to do what your heart tells you.'

'One of our guests—it's a long story—she said I should follow my heart and that there's a lot to be said for forgiveness.'

Quinn sat barely hearing as Leila replied; he was lost in
his thoughts. The years had passed other women had come and
gone but he still carried that same torch for Aisling. The flame
had never even so much as flickered. He gazed into his empty glass at the deep red sediment. He should have laid it on
the line when she came back from Crete, but it didn't seem
right with her dad being so sick. He would have felt as though
he were taking advantage of her when she was vulnerable. Instead, he'd tried to show her through his actions. The meals
he'd cooked and brought around to O'Mara's during those dark
days before Brian passed, and then after to try to tempt her into
eating something. It had hurt him almost as much as he knew
she was hurting to see her in so much pain. He'd felt incom-
petent because all he could do was make sure she knew he was
there for her. He hadn't expected Marcus to happen along, but
he had and the window of opportunity had closed. He would
have gladly knocked the bastard flat on his back for what he'd
done to Aisling. Especially when she was still so raw from her
father's death.

At the same time, he'd hated himself for the relief he'd
felt over the wedding not going ahead. He didn't wish that
heartache on her but any eejit could see Marcus and Aisling
weren't right for each other. She'd latched onto him when she'd
been lost, and unsure how to get past her grief for her dad. They

hadn't even been together a year when they got engaged. It had taken every ounce of Quinn's willpower not to tell her she was making a mistake. He'd distanced himself from her rather than say something she might not forgive him for.

Marcus held her back, she was a restrained version of the Aisling he knew when she was around him; her laugh not quite as loud. It had been a long time since he'd seen her throw back her head and laugh like she used to. It had been good to see her enjoying herself tonight. He watched the light play on the cascade of her hair, red and gold glints shimmering like fire. He wouldn't let that window close on him for a second time.

# Chapter 35

It was after midnight when Aisling clambered into the taxi. Alasdair had called it to take her around the corner and home. She hadn't found herself in rags, her taxi didn't turn into a pumpkin, but her feet ached just as much as if they had been encased in glass slippers all evening. She couldn't wait to kick her shoes off and give her tender tootsies a massage. Her ears were ringing with the music they'd jigged along to with the best of them.

It was a miracle she and Leila had been able to get up from the table let alone perform energetic dance moves after the dessert Quinn had produced. Come to think of it, Quinn had been a little subdued after dinner, and he'd barely touched any of the bite-sized sweeties he'd brought out to share. Instead, he'd sat back content to let them snaffle the lot. He hadn't wanted to join them either as they muscled in on the tiny dance area. He'd sunk the rest of the bottle of wine in their absence. It wasn't like him. She'd been having too much fun to notice anything amiss at the time and, scrunching her toes, she felt a guilty pang. A good friend would have noticed.

Maybe he was worried about his mam. He'd said she was doing alright, but the stroke had given the family a shock. She should have asked him instead of twittering on like she had about Marcus. She'd pop around in the next day or so and thank him for a deadly night; she couldn't remember the last time she'd had such a great craic. She'd be sure to ask him then if everything was okay. She settled on that as the driver slammed his door shut and performed a U-turn. His English was stilted and he clearly wasn't in the mood to practice it given the time of night.

It was a miracle she'd managed to dance in her Jimmy Choo's but despite grievous risk to her ankles, she'd forgotten all about them as she threw herself into the mix. She never could resist a tin pipe and a fiddle. The music was catchy and the atmosphere too infectious not to get in amongst it.

Aisling loved to dance; it made her happy. She'd briefly done ballet as a little girl, but she didn't have the physique to be a ballerina—too sturdy and she'd joined the Brownies for a brief stint instead. Her dancing over the years had been relegated to sticky floors after dark with her friends until Leila had talked her into going along to salsa classes. She rested her head back on the seat and closed her eyes as the conversation between her and Quinn replayed. Why had she never gone back for a second class? She'd loved the initial one the three of them had attended. Not just because she'd met Marcus but because the music had made her feel carefree like she was connecting with another part of herself. A part that wasn't sensible and bound by duty. Why then had she felt because it wasn't Marcus's thing it couldn't be hers either?

She massaged her temples. She was knackered; last night's broken sleep had caught up with her. The second wind she'd been running on had well and truly blown itself out now. The taxi pulled up outside O'Mara's which was in darkness. Aisling paid her fare and the driver waited until she'd let herself in. She locked the door behind her and stepped out of her shoes, her sigh of relief an audible hiss in the deserted reception. As she tiptoed through the inky interior, she passed by Room 1 and wondered whether Una had come back. She might have decided to stay at Aideen's. She'd have to wait until the morning to find out. She was looking forward to hearing how the rest of the day's catching up had panned out for the sisters and what their plans were now they'd reconnected.

The stairs creaked as she made her way up them despite her best efforts to be quiet. Although, fair play to her, she was getting quite good at this creeping about nocturnally business. She unlocked the door to the apartment expecting to have to pat around the wall for the light switch but Moira, uncharacteristically considerate, had left a lamp on for her. She would long since be tucked up in bed Aisling thought, tempted to head straight for her own bed.

Her stomach rolled over reminding her of the evening's excesses. What was it Mammy swore by for digestion problems? Bicarbonate of soda dissolved in warm water sprang to mind. She'd see if that would do the trick. It certainly wouldn't do any harm. So she opened the cupboard where the baking things, that hadn't seen the light of day since Maureen O'Mara had moved out, were kept. There was a tin labelled bicarb—Mammy was a good labeller—tucked at the back which she dug out. She hoped making up the potion it hadn't expired in 1990 or some other decade. It didn't taste flash, punishment for all the rich food she'd shovelled down earlier, but she got it down.

She forced herself into the bathroom to remove her makeup, not fancying waking up with her eyes glued together with the evening's mascara. At last, face washed and teeth brushed, she crept into her bedroom and tossing back the covers clambered in all set to snuggle down and visit the land of nod. Aisling's scream a second later as she felt a warm arm drape itself across her middle should have brought the Guards rushing to their door.

# Chapter 36

'Aisling, for the love of God it's me, Mammy! Shut up.'
    'Jaysus, Mammy,' Aisling rasped, clutching her chest. 'What're you doing?'

'Having a heart attack that's what. I'm getting too old for shocks like that. I didn't know what was going on.'

'If anyone's having palpitations, it's me. I didn't know you were there. You could have been anyone.'

'Who were you expecting to find in yer bed then?'

'Not you!'

Light flooded the room and Aisling and Maureen blinked at Moira looking wild eyed as she stood in the doorway clutching her bedside lamp blinking back at them. 'What the feck is going on? I thought one of you was being murdered.'

They both pointed at each other and said, 'It was her fault.'

'Why're you holding your lamp?' Aisling asked.

'It was the only thing I could find to clobber yer one with.'

'What one?'

'The one who was after sneaking into your room.'

'But it was Mammy.'

'For feck's sake, Aisling, I know that now.'

'Well, I wish one of you had thought to tell me what was going on. Why didn't you go in Patrick's room, Mammy?'

'Ah, the bed's too hard for my back, yours is nice and soft.'

'Who do you think you are? Goldilocks?'

'Shut up you two,' Moira muttered.

Aisling began to calm down and rationale set in. 'I suppose we better check none of the guests were disturbed. We don't want anyone calling the Guards. We'll have everybody up then if they start hammering on the front door. Come on.' They could jolly well come with her, she'd done enough skulking about in the dark as it was, and her poor heart couldn't stand any more shocks like the one she'd just had.

Maureen borrowed Aisling's dressing gown and she threw an oversized cardigan on over top of her nighty while Moira, in her pyjamas, once more led the way.

'If I break my neck getting about in the dark like this—'

'Shush, Mammy,' Aisling threw over her shoulder. A beat later she nearly smacked into the back of Moira which would have sent her toppling down the stairs. She steadied herself focussing on what it was that had brought her up short. A seemingly biblical apparition was illuminated by the light shining from Room 6's open door. At the sight of the wiry old man with the halo of silvery hair and wispy beard, Maureen began to cross herself.

'Jesus, Mary, and Joseph,' she whispered, peering around Aisling's shoulder. She could read Mammy's mind and before she began reciting Hail Mary's, Aisling said, 'It's Branok Nancarrow, Mammy. He and his wife are staying with us. They're from Cornwall, not Jerusalem. Jesus Christ hasn't come calling.' She could almost feel the air go out of Mammy.

'I was thinking more Moses than Jesus for your information.'

Branok looking decidedly rumpled peered up at the three women huddled together near the top of the stairs. 'What's going on? We heard a scream.' From around the door peeped a bleary-eyed, Emblyn.

Aisling stepped forward. 'We're so sorry to have woken you and Emblyn, Branok. It was me you heard and we're fine. Mammy here gave me a fright that's all.'

Maureen pushed her way past Aisling and Moira and headed down the stairs. 'Maureen O'Mara, former proprietor come to spend the night with her girls. How-do-ye-do?'

Branok shook her hand a little taken aback by this bold greeting given the late hour. Emblyn stayed where she was watching the proceedings.

'The girls have always been prone to dramatics but Aisling, well she should have been on the stage.'

'Mammy! That's not fair you were in my bed.'

Branok looked from mother to daughter, bewilderment on his face. 'But everybody's alright that's the main thing.'

Chastened, Aisling marched down and took hold of Mammy's elbow. 'We are, thank you, Branok, and again we're so sorry to have disturbed you and Emblyn.' She flashed an apologetic look at his wife. 'We'll leave you both in peace. Goodnight.'

Branok said there was no harm done and bade them goodnight.

'Don't pull my arm, so,' Maureen said as Aisling herded her up the stairs.

She was not apologetic, nor did she loosen her grip. This was not the time for polite conversation with their guests. She'd be asking what Branok did for a living next and God help them all if she found out he and Emblyn were artists. There'd be no stopping her then, she'd be asking for tips on her latest watercolour. No, she needed to be taken back upstairs.

As she stepped back inside the apartment, Aisling wasn't sure if it was a good thing or not only two guests bothering to get up. She could have been being attacked for all anyone knew. Ah well, she yawned, at least Moira and her lamp had come to her rescue. 'I'll take Patrick's bed tonight, Mammy,' she said, taking herself off to her brother's old room before there could be any argument.

~

Aisling was asleep within minutes of her head hitting the pillow. It was a fitful sleep filled with dreams that made her toss and turn. Marcus was in their dining room, he was dressed in the suit she'd always hated. The one that didn't sit right around his bum and he was holding a slip of paper. She was in the room too only she was tall and willowy. She'd transformed into Maria Lozano. She strutted toward him, the most fabulous pair of pink Louboutin pumps on her feet, beckoning him to join her in a dance of love. He shook his head and waved the paper at her, he was angry. What was on the paper? She peered closer and realised it was her American Express bill. It had angry red circles on it. He threw the paper down, sat on the sofa, and picking up the remote he switched the television on. The last thing Aisling remembered from the dream when she opened her eyes and realised morning had arrived, was he'd been watching the Crocodile Hunter.

She sat up in bed, eyes wide with sudden clarity. She knew exactly what she had to do.

# Chapter 37

Moira had left for work by the time Mammy made an appearance. Aisling was showered and dressed, sitting at the table eating her toast with relish. The weight she'd been carrying since Marcus's letters had begun arriving, had lifted. She'd made her mind up as to what she was going to do where he was concerned and the strawberry jam she'd dolloped on her toast tasted all the sweeter for it.

'I'll have a cuppa and get myself sorted. I'm looking forward to saying hello to everyone, then I'll be away. I've a painting class at twelve. I'm working on a representation of the pier. I think it'll look fetching in reception once I've finished it.'

Representation didn't bode well, Aisling thought.

'Now the rain's gone off, I might squeeze in a round of golf later, too. Derbhilla's getting about much better now. She's stopped hobbling about like a cowboy at high noon. Aisling, where've you gone and put the teabags?'

'Nowhere. They're in the cupboard where they always are. Put your glasses on.'

Mammy enjoyed breezing into O'Mara's. She was greeted like a retired Hollywood star each time, even if it'd only been a matter of weeks since she'd last called in.

Aisling finished her toast, debated another slice but decided that would be greedy, and getting up carried the plate through to the kitchen. She retrieved the sugar bowl and put the milk on the bench too before Mammy could ask where they were. 'I'm going downstairs now. There's a guest I want to check on. I'll see you in a while.'

Mammy was only half listening. 'I think I might see if Mrs Flaherty can spare me a nice sausage and egg. I haven't had a cooked breakfast for ages. Alright if I borrow a pair of clean knickers? Moira's won't fit.'

Charming. She wasn't pinching her expensive Agent Provocateur panties. 'I'll leave a pair on the bed for you,' Aisling said—the old pair from Marks & Spencer she'd been meaning to chuck out should do the trick.

She headed down the stairs and called out good morning to Bronagh. She waved her cereal spoon by way of return greeting and Aisling carried on to the kitchen. Room 1's closed door gave no clue as to whether Una was in there or not and she was eager to see if she was having breakfast. Mrs Flaherty had other ideas, accosting her in the doorway and blocking her view of the dining room.

'That fecking fox has been again.'

'Oh dear.'

'Oh dear, indeed. The bin lid was lying on the ground and he's left a trail of rubbish. I tell you, Aisling, I won't be responsible for my actions if I get hold of him.'

'Fair play, Mrs Flaherty. I'll see what can be done about him, shall I?'

They both knew full well this wouldn't happen, but Mrs Flaherty felt better for having sounded off. She leaned forward giving Aisling a whiff of bacon fat. 'Oh, and, Aisling,' her voice dropped to a conspiratorial whisper. 'You'll never believe it.'

'What?'

'Yer woman from Room 1. Her with the face that only a mother could love over there at the corner table, complimented me on my white pudding this morning. She said it was the best she'd ever had. Went so far to say it was an art form getting the outside as golden and crispy as I managed to yet making sure the inside still stayed creamy and melted in your mouth. Well, I don't mind telling, you could have blown me down with a feather.'

It would take a lot more than a feather to knock Mrs Flaherty down. A bulldozer might do the trick thought Aisling as she smiled, 'Compliments where compliments are due. Don't I always say you're a wonder in the kitchen?'

Mrs Flaherty's apple cheeks flushed with pride and she toddled happily back to the kitchen, fox forgotten. The way was clear for Aisling to make a beeline for Una.

The older woman put her cup down as Aisling approached and beamed at her pushing her chair back.

'Don't get up, Una.' Aisling pulled out the chair opposite her and sat down. 'I'm so glad I found you. I've been desperate to know how the rest of your day with Aideen went.'

Una looked different, younger, brighter, and the pinched expression was gone. She looked how Aisling felt and she wondered if she looked different this morning too.

Una reached across the table and took Aisling's hand in hers, holding it tight. 'I've got my sister back, thanks to you, dear.'

'Oh, it wasn't thanks to me. I didn't do anything.'

'You did more than you'll ever know.'

'Well, you helped me too.'

They smiled at each other and Una gave her hand a final squeeze before releasing it. 'It's been decided. I'm moving in with Aideen. I want to be there to help while she has the rest of her treatment. It will take a load off the boys' shoulders too. They've their own families to be thinking of and I want to spend every second I can with my sister.'

'That's wonderful, Una. It means I'll get to see you again after you check out today too.'

'I'd like that. I'd like that very much. Now then, what's got you looking like the cat that got the cream this morning?'

'I've made my mind up where Marcus is concerned. It came to me this morning, clear as day. I had this dream you see and now I know what I've got to do.'

# Chapter 38

A isling left Una to pack and headed back upstairs. There was no time for her morning check to see the cogs of O'Mara's were turning as they should be, she had a phone call to make. She heard voices as she reached the landing. It was Ita and Mammy; they were in Room 5 and she couldn't help peeking in on them. Mammy was perched on the chair by the window asking after Ita's mam while Ita whipped the sheets off and remade the bed faster than Aisling had ever seen her undertake any task before. Perhaps she should get a cardboard cut-out of Mammy and stand it in the entrance of the rooms she was supposed to be making up.

Carrying on up the stairs she knew when Maureen ventured down to reception she and Bronagh would embrace like it had been years, not mere weeks since they'd last seen each other. 'She's only come from Howth, Bronagh, not New Zealand.' Aisling had said the last time she'd witnessed this carry on.

'Sure look it, Aisling, you don't work for someone for thirty years without missing them when you don't see them on a daily basis anymore.'

'Fair play,' Aisling had said.

She let herself back into the apartment and for a moment, only a moment, wished Mammy would move back in. The place was sparkling. She cast her eyes about before picking up the phone to dial the number she knew by heart.

~

The sky was a moody canopy as she followed the path through the Green. The grey clouds were left over from the downpour the day before but there were patches of blue gallantly appearing. A duck quacked and waddled across the path in front of her and Aisling shivered as a sudden gust sent leaves floating down around her. She was glad she'd thought to put her coat on as her boots crunched over the leaf laden path. Marcus was there already Aisling saw as she approached the bandstand. A lone tourist was trying to capture an arty shot of it, her photo ruined by a man with a newspaper tucked under his arm striding in front of the line of her lens.

Aisling's resolve faltered momentarily at the sight of him. It would have been easier to do this over the phone, take the easy way out, but that wasn't her style. It was his. He waved out and began to walk toward her. The lightness in his step told her how he thought this conversation was going to go. Her insides tightened. *You can do this, Aisling*.

'Hi, you're a sight for sore eyes.' Reaching her, he leaned in and kissed her cheek. How formal, she couldn't help but think as he said, 'It's so good to see you.' He took a step back and thrust his hands in his pockets eyeing her speculatively. 'You said you were ready to talk.'

She managed a watery smile but hesitated trying to find the right words. She'd had no time to rehearse what she wanted to say.

Marcus cut to the chase, forcing her hand. 'Have you had time to think about what I said?' The anticipation of her expected response flickered in his eyes.

For a moment Aisling wobbled. He'd hurt her, but she had no wish to do the same to him. This wasn't a case of tit for tat. 'I've done nothing but.' There was no point in playing games, she breathed in sharply. 'Marcus, I'm sorry. We can't go back. It won't work.'

For a brief second, he looked as though he'd been slapped. It was clearly not what he'd expected to hear. 'But I love you, Ash.'

He looked like a lost little boy, and it wasn't easy to summon what needed to be said. 'I loved you too but you don't love me, Marcus. Not properly. You love who you want me to be.' The past tense slipped easily from her mouth because she knew it was true. Somewhere along the line this last year she'd moved on. She just hadn't known it.

She wanted to be the girl she'd been before Dad died and before she met Marcus. She wanted to be the girl who bought shoes on a whim again—okay maybe not Louboutin's, but she'd find a compromise. She wanted to take dance classes and leave her inhibitions at the door. She wanted to throw her head back and laugh from deep down inside her belly. She'd never laughed like that with Marcus, he'd have found it loud and embarrassing. Quinn didn't, he found it infectious joining in with her. This wasn't about him though.

There were no rewind buttons in life. She couldn't go back, she couldn't change Dad not being here. Nor could she undo the rippling effect grief had, but she could be a new version of her old self. The only way to do that was to keep moving forward.

'I don't get it.'

'I know, but you will. We weren't right for each other Marcus, we're too different. You say *tomato* I say *tomahto*.' She put her hand to her mouth. Where on earth had the Fred Astaire and Ginger Rogers lyric come from? Alasdair sprang to mind.

It had gone over Marcus's head. He was looking at the sycamore leaves settling around his feet. He raised his gaze to meet Aisling's, she didn't flinch. 'You mean it don't you?'

'I do. I won't be changing my mind, Marcus.'

'There's nothing else to say then is there?'

She shook her head, a lump forming in her throat. 'Only that I wish you well.' She meant it. It felt good to finally let go of the anger she'd kept such a tight hold of this past year.

He reached out and touched her face, his fingers brushing the same spot where his lips had grazed her cheek in greeting. 'I wish you all the best too, Ash. No more saying I'm sorry.'

'No more.'

'Well, that's something.' His smile was sad.

'Goodbye, Marcus.'

She turned and walked away not wanting him to see her tears as she strode back down the path.

*Dear Aisling,*

*Today, I said goodbye to my ex-fiancé. He wanted us to try again, but I blamed him for calling our wedding off and leaving me in the lurch. I can see now he did me a favour. We weren't meant to be together. We're too different. So not going back was the right thing to do. The thing is I don't know how to move on from the person I've loved all along. How can I switch off my feelings for someone who's only ever seen me as a friend?*

*Yours faithfully,*

*Me*

~

Quinn marched up the stairs to the first-floor studio. He'd phoned ahead, and the Lozanos were expecting him. He was pulling out all the stops. He wasn't going to lose Aisling to Marcus a second time. If this all blew up in his face, at least he'd know he'd given it his best shot.

# Chapter 39

Reception was quiet when Aisling stepped back inside the guest house. There was no sign of Mammy. Bronagh, barely visible above the desk and with a custard cream halfway to her mouth, read her mind.

'Maureen left twenty minutes ago. She had a painting class she needed to get back for. Oh, and Quinn phoned while you were out too.' For no reason Aisling could fathom other than Bronagh having said his name, she giggled. 'He left a message, said it was very important you get it.'

Aisling was curious. She took the piece of paper Bronagh handed her and read it with a frown. He wanted her to meet him at seven pm at the Lozano's Dance Studio. There was no explanation as to why. She folded the slip of paper and sighed—what a day this one was turning out to be.

'Isn't that the place you did the salsa class, where you met you know who?'

'It is. I only went the once, and I have no idea why Quinn would want to meet there. Maybe I'll give him a call.' She wasn't in the mood for cryptic messages.

'Ah, well now, he also said if you mentioned calling him to try to find out what he was up to, I was to tell you not to. He said, and I'm quoting, *Tell her it's a surprise and a surprise can only be a surprise if she doesn't know what it is.*'

Aisling's frown deepened, what was he up to?

Bronagh's eagle eye noted the smudge of mascara beneath Aisling's eyes and she put her custard cream down. 'Is everything alright?'

'It's going to be, so long as you pass me one of those custard creams.'

'What custard creams?'

'Don't play innocent with me. The packet you keep in your drawer.'

'They're for emergencies only, but looking at the state of yer, I'd say you qualify. Pull up a chair and tell me what's been going on.'

Aisling did as she was told, thinking Bronagh must have an awful lot of emergencies as she helped herself to a biscuit. When she got to the part where she'd told Marcus there was no going back. Bronagh clapped her hands and said she could have the rest of the packet.

Somehow, she managed to fill the day, her eyes straying to the clock every so often, counting down the hours. Her mind kept drifting to the different scenarios as to what Quinn was up to as she tried to run through the accounts. With a sigh she put them aside, they could wait until tomorrow, she'd only make a mess of them if she kept at it today. In the end, she figured he'd booked them back into the dance classes after their conversation at dinner last night. It made sense but what didn't make sense was the secrecy.

Moira, breezing in after work, was a welcome diversion.

'God, I was knackered today after your and Mammy's carry on last night.' She flopped down on the sofa kicking her runners off. 'I kept putting calls through to the wrong person and I got caught with my gob full of egg sandwich by Aiden O'Dwyer.'

'Aiden O'Dwyer's one of Mason Price's clients?' She had Aisling's attention, the man had starred in several Hollywood blockbusters. He was blue eyed, square jawed, dark haired and always played damaged sort of people.

'Ah, he's not all that great,' said Moira. 'He needed a shave and he was wearing green joggers. Green for feck's sake and it's not even St Paddy's. But still, it was embarrassing the sanger got stuck on the roof of my mouth and I couldn't get my words out properly. He'd have thought me a right eejit.'

Aisling grinned at the picture painted.

Moira was moving on in her usual hurricane Moira manner. 'You haven't seen the dress I bought to wear to Posh Mairead's bash yet have you?' She didn't wait for a reply and bounced off the sofa. 'I'll put it on and give you a twirl.'

She reappeared a few minutes later and strutted her stuff through the living room. The dress was a clinging, deep cerise with spaghetti straps, which finished just above her knees. It was sexy but not in an overt way and Aisling gave a low whistle.

'Wow, Moira, you look gorgeous.'

'Shelbourne gorgeous?'

'Savoy, Ritz, Four Seasons gorgeous.'

~

Dinner was a hit and miss affair of heated up leftover Chinese. Aisling wasn't hungry. The half pack of custard creams had seen to that. Besides she was too fidgety and antsy to eat. She hadn't mentioned Quinn's message to Moira knowing she'd be in for a derisive snort at the mention of salsa. She did, however, inform her as to what she'd said to Marcus earlier in the day.

To her surprise, Moira hugged her long and hard. 'I knew you weren't a total eejit.' Now, that was the Moira she knew and loved!

'I'm heading out to meet Quinn at seven. Will I leave it to you to tell Mammy and Roisin, Marcus won't be around anymore?' Aisling said as she headed toward her bedroom.

Moira looked delighted by the prospect as she nodded enthusiastically then registering what she'd said about meeting Quinn said, 'Do you know, Ash, I've always thought Quinn had the glad eye for you.'

It was Aisling who paused and gave the derisive snort. 'No way. We're friends that's all.'

Moira let it be, eager to begin burning up the phone lines with her breaking news.

Aisling stared into her wardrobe. The red dress or the LBD? She held both out and opted for the red, Moira said it gave her a look of a short Nicole Kidman. As for the shoes, she chose her Valentino sling back sandals. They were made for dancing. Ignoring her sister's raised eyebrows she swept through the living room and out the front door. She could imagine the turn the conversation she was having had just taken *'Rosie you want to see the state of her, she's in the red dress. Yes, the shag-me, short Nicole Kidman one. And... she's meeting Quinn!'*

# Chapter 40

Aisling slammed the taxi door shut and stared up at the building. The first floor was in darkness. She knew she wasn't early, not by more than a couple of minutes. She'd left O'Mara's at six forty-five and the traffic had been moving freely. Quinn wouldn't let her down she knew that, so she crossed the street and opened the door. At least the light in the stairwell was on, and she climbed the stairs hearing movement above her. Someone was up there then.

Maybe it was a new thing, salsa in the dark? She pushed open the door expecting to find a few people at least milling about. The room, however, was empty, save for a table draped with a white cloth, a candle flickering in the middle of it. It was laid for two. Her eyes swung to the trolley next to it not understanding. There were several silver tureens and a champagne bucket with a bottle on ice. What on earth was going on?

'Quinn?' she called.

Seemingly from thin air, a fast Latino beat erupted and Quinn emerged from the shadows. It took a few seconds for her eyes to adjust to the dim light and her jaw dropped. This was a version of Quinn she'd never seen before. He was wearing a black open-necked shirt and dress pants as he moved toward her in a cha-cha of triple step forward, right foot back.

Aisling stared in amazement before throwing her head back and laughing. She sobered a beat later as he reached her, and they stood in front of one another. His grin disappeared too and was replaced by something she couldn't fathom.

How was she supposed to be? This was Quinn. The man she'd known since she was eighteen years old. The man she'd hankered after who'd never once looked at her the way he was looking at her now. She could see the question in his eyes as he held his hands out to her. The only sign he was laying it on the line in the slight tremor as she stared at them. They were strong hands, creative hands and if she took them, she'd step off into the unknown. Aisling took a deep breath and grasped hold of them as tight as she could. He pulled her in toward him.

Surely, he must be able to feel her heart thumping, be aware of how the warmth of his chest against hers was liquefying her insides. She tilted her head to look up at him, searching for clues she was reading this right and he was about to kiss her. She decided to be bold and on her tippy toes she sought his lips as he leaned down to find hers, grazing the side of each other's mouths by mistake. That's what happened when old friends crossed a line; Aisling's face was hot but Quinn just laughed. It made her laugh. He made her laugh, he always had.

'Shall we try again?' he asked. 'See if we can get it right this time?'

She nodded.

This time their lips found each other and as Aisling melted in to him, she knew she'd gotten her happy ending, after all.

Hi! I hope this first instalment in The Guesthouse on the Green series made you smile, or even better laugh out loud. If you enjoyed Aisling's story then leaving a short review on Amazon would be wonderful and so appreciated. You can keep up to date with news regarding this series via my newsletter (I promise not to bombard you!) and as a thank you receive an exclusive O'Mara women character profile!

www.michellevernalbooks.com[1]

# Moira Lisa Smile

Book 2, The Guesthouse on the Green

A GIRL WITH A MONA Lisa smile, a woman who wants to confront her demons and that pesky red fox...

Take a break you'll never forget at O'Mara's Manor House with Moira Lisa, Book 2 in the fresh new series - The Guest House on the Green where a full Irish breakfast is always included!

Moira O'Mara's developed an annoyingly enigmatic, Mona Lisa smile of late when it comes to talking about her new man. She's not ready to share him with her family, not just because they treat her like a baby. Look at the way they go on at her about her drinking? It's not a problem, she likes a party, who doesn't? No, he's her secret, and for now, it has to stay that way, but keeping secrets can be hard and knowing when you've gone too far can be even harder.

---

1. http://www.michellevernalbooks.com

When Tessa Delaney was a teenager, her family left Dublin behind, emigrating to New Zealand. She was glad to leave behind the bully who tormented her school days. She knows only too well the old saying of sticks and stones may break my bones but words can never hurt me isn't true. She's booked into the guesthouse determined to confront her teenage years and erase those words for good.

Meanwhile, the little red fox who raids the bins outside O'Mara's basement kitchen door at night is waiting, ready to pounce when Mrs Flaherty tosses out a nice sausage or sliver of white pudding.

Witty, sad, and insightful with a touch of romance. Come and stay at O'Mara's.